USBORNE SCIENCE & EXPERIMENTS
PLANET EARTH

Fiona Watt
Edited by Corinne Stockley
Designed by Stephen Wright

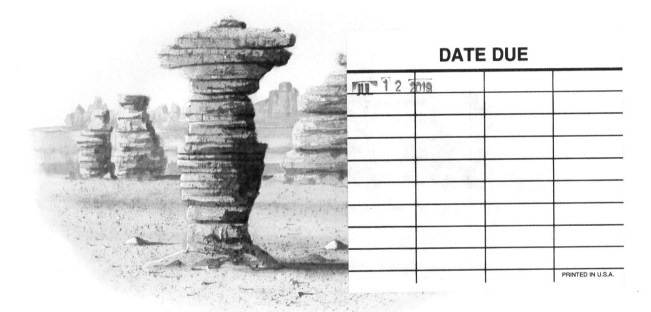

Illustrated by Kuo Kang Chen, Chris Shields and Aziz Khan
Scientific advisors: Steve Stone and Mike Collins

Contents

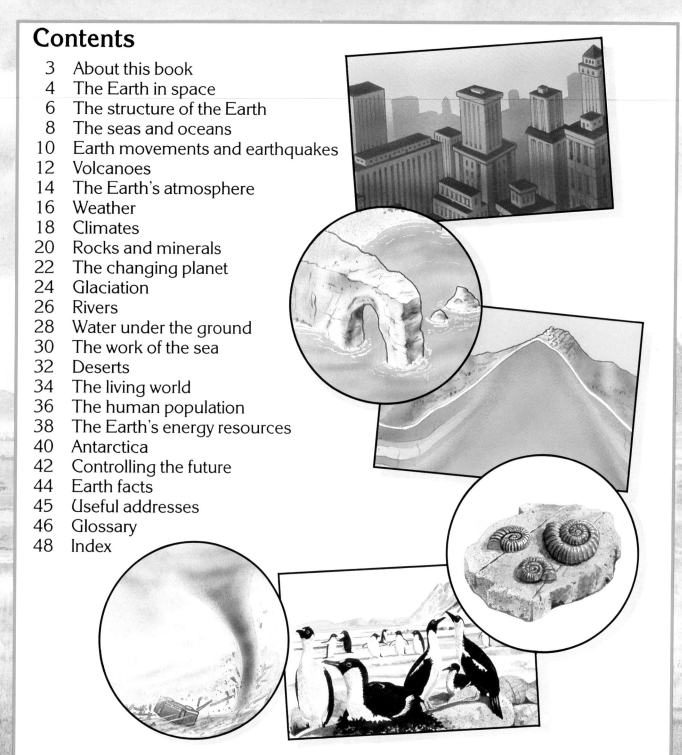

First published in 1991 by Usborne Publishing Ltd, Usborne House, 83-85 Saffron Hill, London EC1N 8RT, England.

Copyright © 1991 Usborne Publishing Ltd.

The name Usborne and the device are Trade Marks of Usborne Publishing Ltd.

Printed in Spain

About this book

The Earth has gradually changed over millions of years to become the complex planet we know today. This book explains how many of the Earth's features and landscapes were formed, such as volcanoes, glaciers and deserts. It also looks at the various processes which continue to shape the Earth's surface, such as the action of rivers, the sea and the weather.

Throughout the book there are examples of many ways in which we use the Earth's resources, such as coal, minerals and energy from the Sun. It also shows the fragile balance which exists between the natural world and human activities. It looks at a wide variety of plant and animal species and how they survive in different environments around the world.

Using the glossary

The glossary on pages 46-47 is a useful reference point. It gives detailed explanations of the more complex terms used in the book, and introduces some new ones.

Useful addresses

On page 45, there is a list of addresses of museums and organizations who may be able to provide you with more information about the Earth and its resources.

Activities and projects

Special boxes like this one are found throughout the book. They are used for experiments and activities which will help you to understand different aspects of physical geography.

All the experiments and activities have clear instructions and are easy to do. You may need to buy some of the equipment at an electrical or hardware shop.

This scene shows an African grassland, or savannah, and some of the many species of animal which live there. Few people live in these areas because the climate is not suitable for farming. For more information about different climates, see page 19.

The Earth in space

The planet Earth seems enormous to us, but it is really just a tiny part of the Universe. The Universe consists of billions of stars, planets and moons, as well as vast areas of emptiness. No one knows how big it is, and astronomers think it is still expanding. They believe it was formed about 20,000 million years ago when all the matter, which was once packed together in one place, was thrown into space by a massive explosion. Galaxies formed in the clouds of dust and gas which spread out. It is thought that the Earth was formed about 4,600 million years ago.

Galaxies, stars and planets

A galaxy is an enormous cluster of thousands of millions of stars and planets. Galaxies can be different shapes, such as spirals. There are over 6,000 million known galaxies.

The Milky Way is a small part of one galaxy, but it is still made up of millions of stars and planets. It has a disc-like shape, formed by 'arms' spiralling out from a central cluster of stars.

The Solar System is a very tiny part of the Milky Way. It is made up of the Sun and the nine major planets. Each planet follows its own elliptical (oval-shaped) path, or orbit, around the Sun. Thousands of asteroids (balls of ice, dust and gas), also travel around the Sun.

The Earth is the fifth largest planet in the Solar System. From space it appears as a blue planet, covered with swirling clouds.

The Universe is so enormous that distances cannot be measured in the normal way, so they are measured in light years. One light year is the distance light travels in a year (9,500 billion kilometres).

The Sun is the centre of the Solar System. It is a not a planet, but a star. Stars send out light and heat energy. This is produced by chemical changes in the very centre, or core, of the star.

The temperature and pressure in the core of the Sun are so high that hydrogen gas is turned into helium gas, giving off huge amounts of energy.

Mercury. Extremely hot, about 500°C in the daytime and −175°C at night. Almost no atmosphere. Rocky surface.

Earth. Temperature range of 60°C to −90°C. Atmosphere of mainly nitrogen and oxygen. 75% of surface covered by water.

Venus. Very hot, about 480°C. Thick, dense atmosphere – clouds of carbon dioxide which trap Sun's heat. Rocky, cratered surface.

Mars. Freezing temperatures. Atmosphere mainly carbon dioxide. Red, rocky surface.

Asteroids. Irregular-shaped lumps of rock which travel around the Sun.

The spinning planets

As each planet orbits the Sun, it rotates about its axis (an imaginary line running through it). The Earth spins around once every 23 hours and 56 minutes. Venus takes 243 Earth days to rotate, whereas Uranus takes only 11 hours.

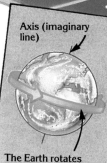

Axis (imaginary line)

The Earth rotates in this direction.

Exploring the planets

Exploration by unmanned space craft, such as the American space probes Viking and Voyager and the Russian probe Venera, has revealed information about the surface and atmosphere of the planets in the Solar System. From the information sent back from space, scientists have worked out what it may be like on each planet.

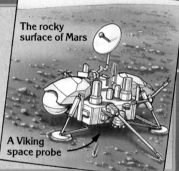

The rocky surface of Mars

A Viking space probe

Pluto. Smallest planet. Thought to have no atmosphere and thick icy crust surrounding core.

Neptune. Receives little light from Sun, so extremely low temperatures. Thought to have rocky core covered in ice crust.

Jupiter. Largest planet, mostly made up of clouds of gas and ice crystals. Atmosphere of hydrogen and helium. Tiny particles and rocks form a ring around it.

Uranus. Blue-green planet due to atmosphere of methane. Very low temperatures. May have solid core. Nine known rings circle the planet.

Saturn. Enormous ball of hydrogen and methane gas, with solid core. Circled by rings of thousands of blocks of ice.

The unique planet

The Earth is the only known planet where living things, as we know them, can exist. It is neither too hot nor too cold and contains just the right mixture of gases and water needed by plants and animals.

The Earth's atmosphere is the only one to contain nitrogen and oxygen. Living things need to breathe or absorb oxygen and nitrogen to build their cells. The atmosphere also helps to reflect harmful radiation from the Sun back into space.

Green plants use the Sun's energy to make their own food in a process called photosynthesis. Animals cannot make their food, so they must eat plants, or other animals.

Without the Sun's energy, life on Earth could not exist. The Earth is the only planet in the Solar System which receives the right amount of light and heat to support life.

A tropical rainforest supports thousands of species of plants and animals.

The structure of the Earth

The structure, atmosphere and natural life of the Earth have gradually changed, or evolved, since it was formed. The planet's rocks provide geologists (people who study rocks and their formation) with information about changes to the surface and structure of the Earth.

Inside the Earth

Inside the Earth are several layers of rock. One way scientists have worked out what these are like is by studying shock waves from earthquakes (see pages 10-11).

The crust is a relatively thin layer, between 6km and 70km thick. It is thickest under mountains. The oceanic crust lies below the oceans and runs under the continental crust, which forms the land.

The·inner core is solid and is made from iron and nickel. It is extremely hot (about 5,000°C).

The outer core is made from molten (liquid) metal. As the Earth rotates, this layer moves around very slowly, producing the Earth's magnetic field.

The mantle is the layer of rock below the crust. It is about 3,000km thick. Areas of the mantle are so hot that the rock has melted to form a thick, treacle-like substance called magma (see page 12).

The Earth's crust

Mountains

Ocean

Continental crust

Oceanic crust

Mantle

Continental plates

The Earth's crust is divided into large pieces, or continental plates, which move around very slowly. If they move apart, magma comes up, cools and forms new rock. If they collide, they either rise up, or one is pushed below the other. Plates can also slide sideways against each other.

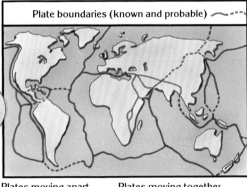
Plate boundaries (known and probable) ∼---

Plates moving apart

Plates moving together

Moving continents

If you look at a world map, you will see that the shapes of the continents seem to match each other like the pieces of a giant jigsaw puzzle. Some scientists think the continents were once joined together (about 200 million years ago), forming one massive land they call Pangea. They think the continental plates gradually drifted apart, making the land split up to form today's continents.

Evidence for the existence of Pangea comes from fossils, the remains of dead plants and animals preserved in rock. Fossils of the same creatures have been found on continents thousands of kilometres apart. For example, fossils of Lystrosaurus, a plant-eating reptile, have been found in South Africa, Asia and Antarctica. This suggests that these continents were once joined.

Some people do not think Pangea ever existed. They say that animals travelled across strips of land, or land bridges, which once existed between the continents. Others think they travelled across the oceans on clumps of floating plants.

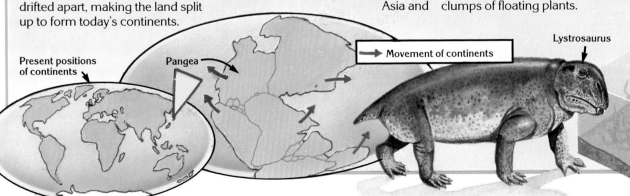

Present positions of continents

Pangea

Movement of continents

Lystrosaurus

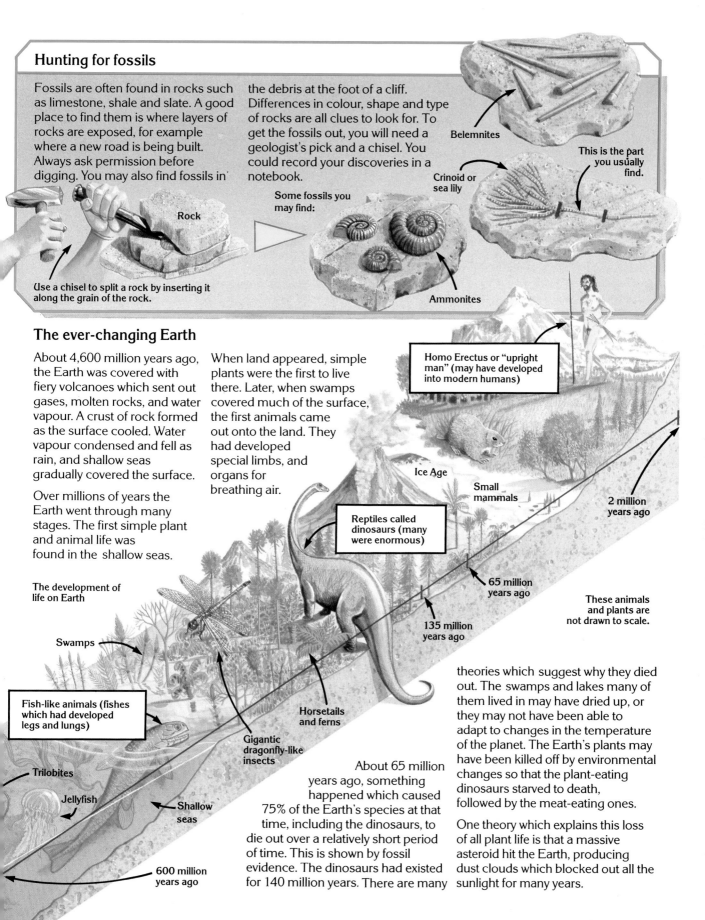

Hunting for fossils

Fossils are often found in rocks such as limestone, shale and slate. A good place to find them is where layers of rocks are exposed, for example where a new road is being built. Always ask permission before digging. You may also find fossils in the debris at the foot of a cliff. Differences in colour, shape and type of rocks are all clues to look for. To get the fossils out, you will need a geologist's pick and a chisel. You could record your discoveries in a notebook.

Belemnites

This is the part you usually find.

Crinoid or sea lily

Use a chisel to split a rock by inserting it along the grain of the rock.

Rock

Some fossils you may find:

Ammonites

The ever-changing Earth

About 4,600 million years ago, the Earth was covered with fiery volcanoes which sent out gases, molten rocks, and water vapour. A crust of rock formed as the surface cooled. Water vapour condensed and fell as rain, and shallow seas gradually covered the surface.

Over millions of years the Earth went through many stages. The first simple plant and animal life was found in the shallow seas.

When land appeared, simple plants were the first to live there. Later, when swamps covered much of the surface, the first animals came out onto the land. They had developed special limbs, and organs for breathing air.

Homo Erectus or "upright man" (may have developed into modern humans)

Ice Age

Small mammals

2 million years ago

Reptiles called dinosaurs (many were enormous)

65 million years ago

135 million years ago

These animals and plants are not drawn to scale.

The development of life on Earth

Swamps

Fish-like animals (fishes which had developed legs and lungs)

Horsetails and ferns

Gigantic dragonfly-like insects

Trilobites

Jellyfish

Shallow seas

600 million years ago

About 65 million years ago, something happened which caused 75% of the Earth's species at that time, including the dinosaurs, to die out over a relatively short period of time. This is shown by fossil evidence. The dinosaurs had existed for 140 million years. There are many theories which suggest why they died out. The swamps and lakes many of them lived in may have dried up, or they may not have been able to adapt to changes in the temperature of the planet. The Earth's plants may have been killed off by environmental changes so that the plant-eating dinosaurs starved to death, followed by the meat-eating ones.

One theory which explains this loss of all plant life is that a massive asteroid hit the Earth, producing dust clouds which blocked out all the sunlight for many years.

The seas and oceans

Almost three-quarters of the Earth's surface is covered by vast oceans and smaller seas. They supply the Earth's atmosphere with water vapour which rises to form clouds (see pages 16-17). They also influence the weather and climates of the world because winds are warmed or cooled as they pass over them.

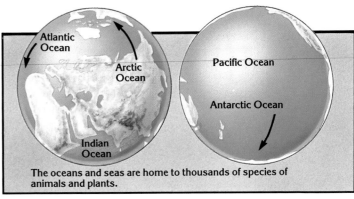

The oceans and seas are home to thousands of species of animals and plants.

The main ocean currents of the world

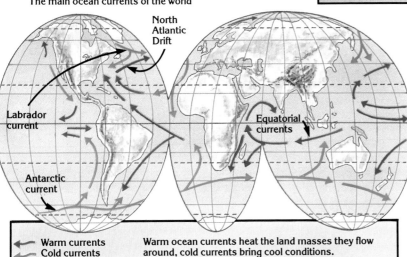

Warm ocean currents heat the land masses they flow around, cold currents bring cool conditions.

Ocean currents

Ocean water travels around the world in currents. Surface currents form as the wind pushes the surface along. They follow the direction of the prevailing winds (the commonest winds which blow in an area). Warm currents flow near the surface where the Sun heats the water. Cold currents flow deep in the ocean, often moving in a different direction to surface currents.

All currents influence the climates of lands in their path. For example, Iceland lies in the flow of the North Atlantic Drift, or Gulf Stream, and is warmer in winter than places further south.

The ocean floor

The ocean floor has many mountains, hills, valleys and deep trenches. Many of the ridges and trenches run along the boundaries of the continental plates.

The longest mountain range in the world, the Mid-Atlantic Ridge, lies in the Atlantic Ocean. Along the ridge, molten rock rises through cracks in the ocean floor and solidifies or hardens, as it meets the cold water.

Deep trenches in the ocean floor occur where one plate disappears below another. The deepest trench, the Mariana Trench in the Pacific Ocean, plunges 11,033m below sea level. If Mount Everest (8,843m) stood in the trench, its summit would still not reach up to the ocean floor.

Tropical cyclones

Warm ocean currents can cause tropical cyclones (called hurricanes in America and typhoons in the Far East). These are fierce storms, with strong winds which form massive waves up to 25m high. The moist, warm air rises and cools, forming clouds.

Cooler air from the ocean surface rushes into the space left by the rising warm air and begins to spiral around. Wind speeds increase and land which lies in the cyclone's path is hit by the fierce storm.

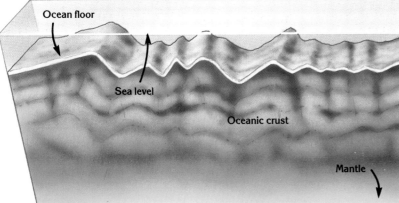

Tropical cyclones can reach 320km per hour

The frozen ocean

In the far north, ice covers much of the Arctic Ocean. When the water freezes, ice forms on the surface. As the wind blows, the ice moves and forms slabs, or floes. These join together to make a field of pack ice, hundreds of kilometres across.

Ships which travel in polar regions have reinforced hulls to cut a path through the ice.

Volcanic islands

Underwater volcanoes are formed when molten rock rises to the surface through cracks in the oceanic crust and solidifies as it comes into contact with the cold, deep ocean water.

Where there are violent eruptions, large amounts of lava build up and the volcanoes appear above the surface as islands.

Surtsey lies on the Mid-Atlantic ridge.

Steam rising as molten rock meets the cold sea.

▲
Off the coast of Iceland, in 1963, fishermen thought they saw a boat on fire. It turned out to be eruptions from an underwater volcano. In just ten days, the volcano grew almost 200m above sea level, forming a new island which was named Surtsey.

Volcanic island

Mountain range

Life in the oceans

Sea water contains oxygen, which is vital for all the animals which live in the oceans. The oxygen comes from seaweeds and phytoplankton (tiny single-celled plants). Like all green plants, these use the Sun's energy to make food, producing oxygen.

Because they need sunlight, all plants live near the surface of the oceans, so most animals live there too, as there is plenty of oxygen and food.

Herring find food in the surface waters of the oceans.

Seaweeds

No light from the surface reaches the depths of the oceans, so plants cannot live there. This means the deep water contains very little oxygen, so the animals which live there have special breathing systems. They feed on debris which falls from the water above.

Some fish have special light cells which they use to attract their prey or to find a mate. Angler fish have a light which dangles above their mouth.

No plants can exist at the bottom of the ocean.

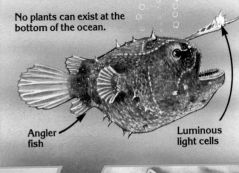

Angler fish

Luminous light cells

Trench

Earth movements and earthquakes

As the Earth's continental plates move together or apart, or slide sideways (see page 6), pressure, or stress, is exerted all across the layers of rocks which make up the plates. Although most rocks are hard, the pressure may cause them either to bend, making wave-like formations called folds, or to break, causing a line of weakness called a fault.

Folds

Folds occur when pressure which builds up in the crust makes the rock crumple up. This may happen at the plate edges or further inside the plates. The crumpled rock may rise to form mountain ranges, such as the Himalayas and the Alps.

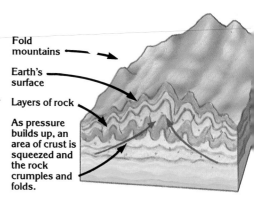

Fold mountains

Earth's surface

Layers of rock

As pressure builds up, an area of crust is squeezed and the rock crumples and folds.

Faults

Faults are cracks, found throughout the crust. The major ones are found at plate boundaries. The main types are normal, reverse and tear faults.

Any movement of the plates has its greatest effect at faults because they are lines of weakness. If the pressure created by the movement is released suddenly, an earthquake may occur. San Francisco and Los Angeles both lie on the San Andreas fault, a tear fault in California.

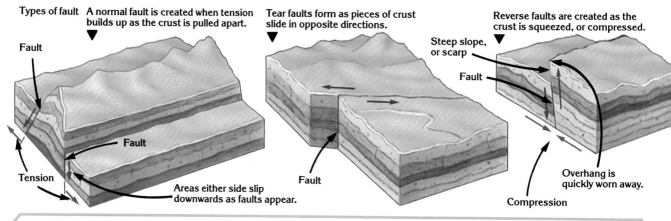

Types of fault A normal fault is created when tension builds up as the crust is pulled apart. ▼

Fault

Fault

Tension

Areas either side slip downwards as faults appear.

Tear faults form as pieces of crust slide in opposite directions. ▼

Fault

Reverse faults are created as the crust is squeezed, or compressed. ▼

Steep slope, or scarp

Fault

Overhang is quickly worn away.

Compression

Making a vibration detector

Earthquake vibrations are detected by special machines. You can make your own vibration detector to use around your home.

What you will need

30cm hacksaw blade
4.5 volt battery
Small light bulb and holder
3x12cm lengths of single core wire (ask for help to strip 2cm at the ends)
Two pieces of wood (approx. 40cm x 10cm x 1cm and 4cm x 2cm x 1.5cm)
A screw
A drawing pin
Strong glue

What to do

1. Stick the small block of wood to the larger piece, as shown.

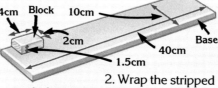

4cm Block 10cm

2cm

Base

40cm

1.5cm

2. Wrap the stripped end of one wire around the screw, and screw one end of the hacksaw blade to the block.

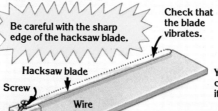

Be careful with the sharp edge of the hacksaw blade.

Check that the blade vibrates.

Hacksaw blade

Screw

Wire

3. Wrap one end of another wire around the drawing pin and push it into the base below the free end of the blade. Attach the other end of the wire to the bulb holder.

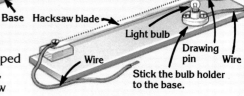

Hacksaw blade

Light bulb

Drawing pin

Wire

Stick the bulb holder to the base.

Wire

4. Attach the last wire to the bulb holder (second connection) and the two loose ends to the battery. When vibrations make the blade touch the pin, the bulb will light.

You may need a weight (e.g. a coin) on the blade, to keep it nearer the pin.

Wire

Battery

Earthquakes

Earthquakes occur when there is a sudden release of pressure, for instance when plates slip suddenly. The point in the crust or upper mantle where this happens is called the focus. Vibrations, or shock waves, pass outwards through the rocks.

Earthquakes have most effect at the epicentre, the point on the surface directly above the focus. They are often followed by weaker aftershocks as the rocks resettle. The areas most likely to suffer are those which lie on plate boundaries.

Every year over 500,000 earthquakes take place, but only a few cause severe damage. It is hard to predict where or when they will occur, although there are some signs which may come before an earthquake, such as a series of small shocks.

Measuring earthquakes

Seismologists (scientists who study Earth movements) use two different scales to measure earthquakes.

The Richter scale is based on the amount of energy produced at the focus. This is worked out using a seismometer, a device which measures surface vibrations. Each step up the Richter scale is about 30 times greater than the last.

The San Francisco earthquake of 1989 measured 7.1. It destroyed sections of the Bay Bridge and made the upper layer of an interstate road collapse.

The Mercalli scale is based on eyewitness observations (see below). The Armenian earthquake of 1988, which destroyed whole towns, rated 10.7 on the Mercalli scale.

The Mercalli scale

1 Not felt.

2 Felt by a few people, and on upper floors of buildings.

3 Hanging objects swing.

4 Windows and objects rattle.

5 Liquids spill, objects fall over.

6 Felt by everyone. Pictures fall off walls, windows break.

7 Difficult to stand, buildings damaged.

8 Towers and chimneys collapse.

9 General panic, cracks appear in the ground.

10 Severe damage to buildings and bridges.

11 Railway lines bend, underground pipes break.

12 Nearly everything damaged, large areas of land slip and move.

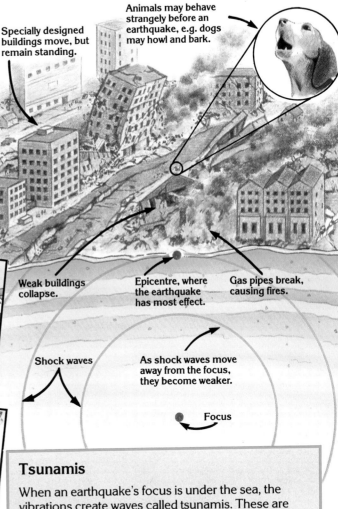

Animals may behave strangely before an earthquake, e.g. dogs may howl and bark.

Specially designed buildings move, but remain standing.

Weak buildings collapse.

Epicentre, where the earthquake has most effect.

Gas pipes break, causing fires.

Shock waves

As shock waves move away from the focus, they become weaker.

Focus

Tsunamis

When an earthquake's focus is under the sea, the vibrations create waves called tsunamis. These are often known as tidal waves, but they are not caused by tides. By the time they reach land they may be many metres high and cause severe flooding.

Tsunamis can cross oceans, causing damage to areas thousands of kilometres away from an epicentre.

Tsunamis up to 30m high can crash onto coasts.

Volcanoes

Volcanoes, like earthquakes, are usually found in areas near the boundaries of continental plates. When pressure builds up below the crust, magma (molten rock) and gas are forced up into weak areas.

The magma may cool and solidify in the crust, or it may break through onto the surface, where it is called lava. It may emerge through thin cracks, called fissures, or be forced out through a wider pipe, where it builds up to form a volcano.

Inside an erupting volcano

Steam, dust and gas rise into the upper atmosphere.

Volcanic blocks and bombs (rock fragments thrown out from the volcano)

Falling ash

Crater

Vent (above ground level)

If the vent is blocked by solidified lava, a secondary cone may form on the side of the volcano.

When magma cools below the surface, dykes or sills may be formed.

Dykes are formed in near-vertical cracks which cut across layers of rock, or strata.

Sills are sheet-like formations which lie along the strata.

The magma rises up the pipe and into the vent.

Pipe (below ground level)

Magma chamber

The shape of volcanoes

The shape of a volcano depends on the type of lava, how far it flows and the strength of the eruption. Viscous lava is thick and sticky, and cools quickly around the vent, solidifying and building up steep-sided cones. Non-viscous lava is thin, runny lava. It may flow for several kilometres before it cools.

When an eruption stops, magma in the vent and crater solidifies, forming a plug. Live volcanoes may be active, erupting fairly frequently, or dormant, resting for a long time between eruptions. Dead, or extinct, volcanoes will not erupt again.

Alternate layers of viscous lava and ash form steep-sided cones, called composite volcanoes.

Shield volcanoes are formed from non-viscous lava. They are low and flat.

Types of eruptions

When pressure builds below the crust, gas and magma explode through the pipe and vent of a volcano. This throws out dust, ash and rocks. Sometimes an eruption will be so violent that the whole volcano blows up, leaving a large crater called a caldera.

Not all eruptions are violent. When the lava is runny, gases escape easily and the lava flows or spurts from the vent.

Shield volcanoes in Hawaii produce spurting fountains of runny lava.

The gases in viscous magma escape with force, causing an explosion in the chamber or pipe. Ash is thrown high into the air.

Predicting volcanic eruptions

It is difficult to predict when an eruption will occur, as each one is different. In the past, certain signs have been noted, such as bulges appearing on the side of a volcano, but nowadays more accurate predictions are possible. Scientists use satellites to detect "hotspots" below the surface.

Hot springs, geysers and fumaroles

In areas of volcanic activity, hot zones of the mantle lie relatively near the surface. Water in the ground is heated by the surrounding hot rocks. It bubbles up through cracks, forming hot springs.

Geysers are springs which send out jets of steam and water under pressure. Volcanic gases are given off from vents in the ground called fumaroles.

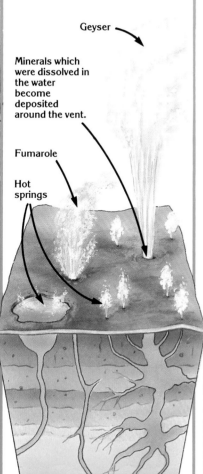

Geyser

Minerals which were dissolved in the water become deposited around the vent.

Fumarole

Hot springs

Hot rocks

Vesuvius

In AD79, Vesuvius, a volcano in Italy, suddenly erupted. Hot ash and poisonous gas spread over nearby towns and cities. One city, Pompeii, lay under 6m of volcanic ash until it was discovered in 1711. The ash had protected the city, preserving the buildings and leaving things exactly as they had been when Vesuvius erupted. Vesuvius has erupted many times since then, but not as violently as in AD79.

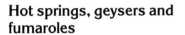

People and animals died as they tried to escape from the ash and sulphur fumes.

Models were made by pouring plaster into the hollows left by the decomposed bodies.

Benefits from volcanoes

Rocks which come from volcanoes are known as igneous rocks (see page 20). Many contain valuable ores and minerals, such as diamonds, gold and copper. Despite the constant threat of eruptions, many people use the fertile soil on the slopes of volcanoes for farming.

Making a model volcano

To make a model volcano which will erupt safely, you will need bicarbonate of soda (sodium bicarbonate), washing-up liquid, three tablespoons of vinegar, red food colouring, a test tube or some other tube-like container, cotton wool and sand or fine soil.

What to do

1. Place a teaspoonful of bicarbonate in the tube. Add warm water so that it is a third full. Shake the mixture thoroughly.

Place your thumb over the end when you shake the mixture.

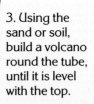

Test tube

2. Add five drops of washing-up liquid and three drops of food colouring (to make your 'lava' look real). Mix the liquid.

Put some cotton wool in the neck of the tube.

3. Using the sand or soil, build a volcano round the tube, until it is level with the top.

The plug stops the sand getting into the mixture.

Sand or soil

Foam 'lava'

4. Remove the plug and pour in the vinegar from a small container. The new mixture will fizz up and out, like lava bubbling from a volcano.

The Earth's atmosphere

The atmosphere is a mixture of gases which surrounds the planet, stretching from the surface to over 900km into space. It protects the Earth from the harmful rays of the Sun and also contains the gases vital to all living things. The atmosphere traps heat from the Sun, warming up the air near the surface and creating the weather.

The composition of the atmosphere

The main gases which make up the Earth's atmosphere are nitrogen (78%) and oxygen (21%). There are also traces of carbon dioxide and other gases. Water exists in the atmosphere as water vapour, as droplets in clouds and as ice crystals.

The layers of the atmosphere

The atmosphere is divided into layers (though there are no sharp boundaries). The temperature changes through the layers (see below – read up from the bottom).

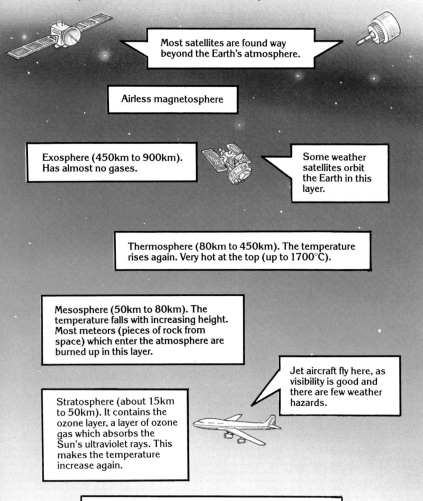

Most satellites are found way beyond the Earth's atmosphere.

Airless magnetosphere

Exosphere (450km to 900km). Has almost no gases.

Some weather satellites orbit the Earth in this layer.

Thermosphere (80km to 450km). The temperature rises again. Very hot at the top (up to 1700°C).

Mesosphere (50km to 80km). The temperature falls with increasing height. Most meteors (pieces of rock from space) which enter the atmosphere are burned up in this layer.

Jet aircraft fly here, as visibility is good and there are few weather hazards.

Stratosphere (about 15km to 50km). It contains the ozone layer, a layer of ozone gas which absorbs the Sun's ultraviolet rays. This makes the temperature increase again.

Troposphere. Varies in height from the surface to between 8km and 15km. Weather forms in this layer, which contains most water vapour, wind and dust. The temperature decreases with height.

Air pressure

Although you cannot feel it, the layers of the atmosphere exert a force, or pressure, on the Earth's surface. Air pressure is greatest on the surface and decreases as you rise through the layers. It is affected by the temperature of the land or sea, so places at the same height do not always have the same pressure. Low pressure often brings wet weather, and high pressure is linked with fine weather.

Making a model barometer

Air pressure is measured on a barometer. To make a model barometer which shows changes in air pressure, you will need a wide-mouthed jar, a balloon, a drinking straw, an elastic band and some card.

What to do

1. Cut the neck off the ▶ balloon and stretch the balloon over the mouth of the jar, so that it is taut.

   Fix the balloon in place with the rubber band.

2. Cut one end of the straw to make a point. Fix the other end to the middle of the stretched balloon using some sticky ▶ tape.

   Straw pointer

   Make sure the straw is horizontal and that it is touching the balloon.

   Sticky tape

3. Place the card behind the jar so that the pointer is touching the card, and mark the position of the pointer. Draw a scale above and below this mark. Tape the card to the jar, with the mark in line with the pointer.

▼

As the air pressure rises, the extra pushing force will push down on the balloon, and the pointer will move up the scale.

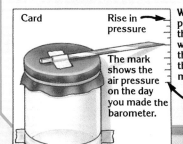

Card

Rise in pressure

The mark shows the air pressure on the day you made the barometer.

When the air pressure falls, the air in the jar will push up on the balloon and the pointer will move down.

Fall in pressure

Movement of air in the atmosphere

Differences in temperature and pressure cause the air in the lower layers of the atmosphere to move, forming the world's winds. They blow from areas of high pressure towards low pressure areas. In many places there are local winds, caused by differences between the temperature of the land and sea. High mountains also affect local winds.

The main pressure belts and winds of the Earth

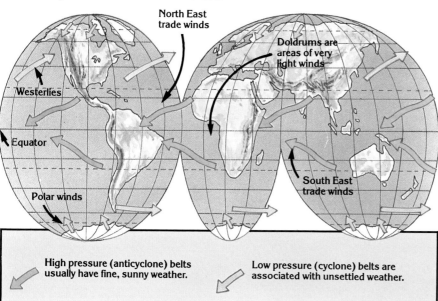

North East trade winds

Doldrums are areas of very light winds

Westerlies

Equator

South East trade winds

Polar winds

High pressure (anticyclone) belts usually have fine, sunny weather.

Low pressure (cyclone) belts are associated with unsettled weather.

The greenhouse effect

Heat energy from the Sun is trapped by carbon dioxide and other gases in the atmosphere. This process is called the greenhouse effect because it occurs in much the same way as glass traps heat in a greenhouse.

The amount of carbon dioxide in the atmosphere is increasing as fossil fuels (see pages 38-39) are burnt. World temperatures are rising as more heat is trapped. This is known as global warming.

Heat and light energy from the Sun enter the atmosphere.

The greenhouse gases trap some of the heat given back out by the Earth, increasing the temperature.

Ozone in the atmosphere

The ozone layer is found in the stratosphere. It is a layer of ozone gas which absorbs much of the Sun's ultraviolet radiation, preventing it from reaching the Earth.

Scientists have found that gases called CFCs (chlorofluorocarbons), destroy ozone gas. They are used in some aerosol cans and refrigerators. Holes have been discovered in the ozone layer above the Arctic and Antarctica. These may increase the amount of ultraviolet radiation which reaches the Earth.

Surface ozone is produced in the lower atmosphere, by a chemical reaction between sunlight and the exhaust fumes from cars. Normally it disperses through the atmosphere, but if a layer of cold air is trapped beneath warm air, it becomes concentrated and causes photochemical smog. Unfortunately, surface ozone cannot replace holes in the higher ozone layer.

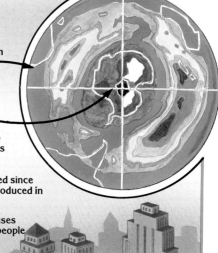

Photographs taken from satellites show the hole in the ozone layer above Antarctica.

The size of the hole changes, but scientists think it is growing.

Efforts are being made to control the exhaust fumes from cars.

Air pollution has decreased since smokeless fuels were introduced in cities.

Photochemical smog causes eye irritations and some people find breathing difficult.

15

Weather

Weather is the daily condition of the atmosphere at a particular place at any one time. It changes from day to day and from place to place and is a combination of temperature, precipitation (rain, snow, sleet or hail), humidity (the amount of water vapour in the air), wind and sunshine. Winds are important as they help to circulate the air in the atmosphere around the world (see page 15).

The seasons

The seasons are caused by the amount of heat and light energy the Earth receives from the Sun. The seasons change due to the way parts of the Earth receive direct sunshine at different times of the year. The Earth is tilted at an angle, and as it orbits the Sun, a different half, or hemisphere, gradually receives more direct sunlight. It is summer in the hemisphere which receives most sunlight and winter in the other. Areas near the equator have no real variations in the seasons. This is because the Sun is almost directly overhead throughout the year.

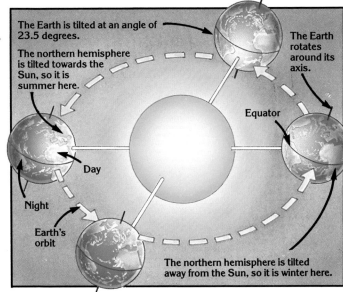

The Earth is tilted at an angle of 23.5 degrees.

The northern hemisphere is tilted towards the Sun, so it is summer here.

The Earth rotates around its axis.

Equator

Day

Night

Earth's orbit

The northern hemisphere is tilted away from the Sun, so it is winter here.

Making a rain detector

To make a detector that will buzz when it rains, you will need some kitchen foil, a clothes peg, a sugar lump, a buzzer, a 4.5 volt battery and 220cm of single core wire cut into 2 x 1m and 1 x 20cm pieces (with 2cm stripped at each end).

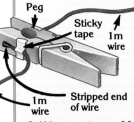

Peg

Sticky tape   1m wire

1m wire

Stripped end of wire

1. Using sticky tape, attach one 1m wire to the gripping end of the peg, without covering the stripped wire. Attach the other 1m wire on the other side.

2. Wrap a piece of foil around each gripping end of the peg to make two contact points. The foil must touch the bare wire.

Peg

Foil contacts

Peg

Foil contacts   1m wire

Terminals

1m wire   Buzzer   20cm wire

Battery

3. Attach one of the 1m wires to the buzzer, and the other to the battery. Join one end of the 20cm wire to the buzzer and the other to the battery. The buzzer should now go off.

4. Put a small piece of a sugar lump between the foil contacts. Put the peg outside and keep the rest of the detector inside. When it rains, the sugar will dissolve and the foil contacts will touch, setting off the buzzer.

The water cycle

When water is heated by the Sun, some of it evaporates. This means it changes into water vapour, which rises and mixes with other gases in the atmosphere. When moist air rises, it cools and the vapour condenses (changes back into a liquid), forming tiny droplets which join to make clouds.

Depending on the air conditions, the water returns to the ground as rain, snow or hail. Snow forms at low temperatures, when tiny ice crystals join together.

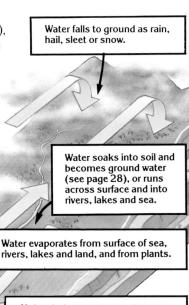

Water falls to ground as rain, hail, sleet or snow.

Clouds rise and cool further. Water droplets get bigger.

Water soaks into soil and becomes ground water (see page 28), or runs across surface and into rivers, lakes and sea.

Water evaporates from surface of sea, rivers, lakes and land, and from plants.

Moist air rises and cools. Water vapour condenses to form clouds.

Clouds

Clouds are found at all levels in the troposphere (see page 14). Their shape, colour and height give clues as to what kind of weather can be expected during the following hours or days. The main types of clouds are cirrus, cumulus and stratus. Not all clouds produce rain, or other forms of precipitation. If clouds move to a warmer area, the water vapour evaporates again.

Cirrus are high level clouds made from ice crystals.

Cumulus clouds may form puffy, fair weather clouds.

Stratus clouds form a thick, low level blanket of cloud, associated with light rain or drizzle.

Hail

Hailstones are small pellets of ice, formed when currents of air lift falling raindrops back to the top of a cloud. The raindrops freeze and receive several coatings of ice as they are carried up and down in the cloud by random air currents. They finally fall as hailstones.

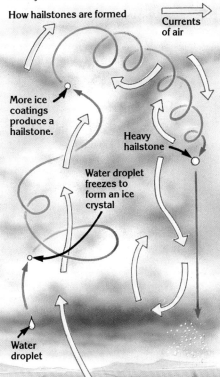

How hailstones are formed

Currents of air

More ice coatings produce a hailstone.

Heavy hailstone

Water droplet freezes to form an ice crystal

Water droplet

Weather hazards

Some types of weather may be very destructive. For instance, unusual amounts of rainfall may result in flooding or droughts. Severe droughts and famine have been experienced in Africa, when seasonal rainfall amounts were low and crops failed.

Floods caused by heavy rain often coincide with gales and high tides. Tropical cyclones (see page 8) cause severe damage, particularly at coasts.

Tornadoes are twisting whirlwinds, formed over land by hot air rising rapidly.

Tornadoes travel across the land, lifting and destroying anything in their path, including trees and cars.

Thunder and lightning

Thunderstorms occur when warm, moist air rises rapidly, forming tall clouds called cumulonimbus. Thunder and lightning are caused by a build-up of different electrical charges within these clouds. Once the charge at the base of the cloud gets to a certain strength, electricity is released as lightning.

Lightning heats the air it travels through and waves of air push outwards. They travel faster than the speed of sound, creating a sonic boom (like a supersonic aeroplane as it passes). This is thunder. Lightning tends to strike a high point, such as an isolated tree or a tall building.

Cumulonimbus cloud

A flash of lightning is actually made up of a number of downward and upward strokes, all occurring within a fraction of a second.

The leader stroke zigzags towards the ground, creating a path of charged air.

The main, return stroke leaps upwards from the ground, along this path. This stroke produces the clap of thunder.

More downward and upward strokes follow.

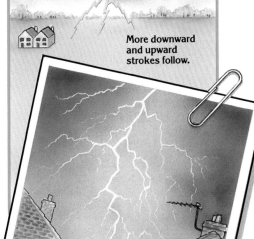

Climates

The climate of an area is the pattern of weather conditions experienced in that area over many years. One type of climate may affect a vast region or a small, local area, where it is called a microclimate.

Climates are affected by the distance from the sea, the altitude (height above sea level) and winds. The climate of an area determines the type of plants and animals found there. It also affects the lifestyle of the people.

Energy from the Sun

Most heat reaches the Earth's surface at the equator, where the Sun is directly overhead. The poles are much colder because the heat is spread over a greater area. The amount of energy any area of the Earth's surface receives from the Sun is called its insolation. Uneven heating of the surface causes movement of air and water vapour throughout the world, forming different climates.

North pole
Atmosphere
Equator
Rays of solar energy
Sun ➝
South pole

Solar energy travels a shorter distance through the atmosphere at the equator than at the poles.

The influence of oceans and seas

Ocean currents influence the climate of any land they pass (see page 8). During the day and at night, the land and sea gain and lose heat at different rates. This makes the air above them move, forming a coastal, or maritime, climate.

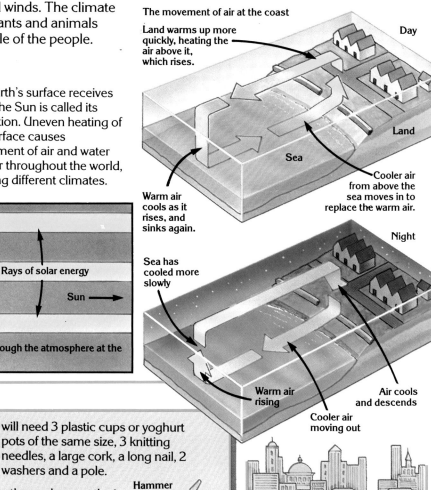

The movement of air at the coast

Land warms up more quickly, heating the air above it, which rises.

Day

Land

Sea

Cooler air from above the sea moves in to replace the warm air.

Warm air cools as it rises, and sinks again.

Sea has cooled more slowly

Night

Warm air rising

Cooler air moving out

Air cools and descends

Urban climates

Cities tend to be warmer than the area surrounding them. This is because concrete absorbs more heat than vegetation and retains it longer, making the nights warmer.

The ground beneath a city tends to be drier, as roads and pavements stop water draining into the soil.

Observing wind speeds

The wind affects the climate of an area. Its speed is measured on an instrument called an anemometer. To make a model anemometer you will need 3 plastic cups or yoghurt pots of the same size, 3 knitting needles, a large cork, a long nail, 2 washers and a pole.

What to do

1. Make two holes in each cup as shown, and push a knitting needle through.

2. Push the points of the needles into the sides of the cork and push the nail down through the centre.

3. Place the washers on the pole, and hammer the nail down through them.

4. On different days, record the number of times the cups spin round in a set time, e.g. 15 seconds. Find out the wind speed from a weather report and make your own wind speed scale.

Loosen the nail if the cork will not turn freely.

You could paint one cup, to help you count the turns.

Knitting needle

Plastic cup

Holes

Nail

Cork

Knitting needle

Hammer

Washers

Nail

Pole

No. of turns Wind speed

Mountain climates

On a mountain, temperatures decrease with altitude, giving different climates and vegetation at different heights. Trees cannot survive on high mountain slopes because there is little soil, which is often covered with snow, and there are frequent high winds. The direction a mountain side or valley faces (its aspect) also affects the climate. One side of a mountain may receive more sunlight than the other, which is nearly always in shadow.

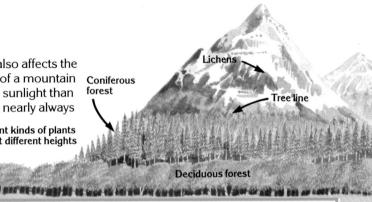

Different kinds of plants grow at different heights

Lichens

Coniferous forest

Tree line

Deciduous forest

Climates of the world

The different climates of the world determine the species of plants and animals found in different areas.

Climates also influence the way people live, their homes and their clothes. Where there are mountains in an area, the lower temperature high up will affect the climate and the types of living things found there.

Major climates of the world

Tundra

Winter temperatures low, averaging from -30°C to -20°C in coldest months. Low rainfall. Rise in temperatures in summer months, may even reach 17°C.

Snow in winter covers low-growing plants, such as lichens.

Polar

Extremely low temperatures with little rain or snowfall, making these icy areas frozen deserts. Animals depend on sea for food, so most wildlife found around coasts.

Animals are insulated by a layer of fat or thick fur.

Temperate

Seasonal variation in temperature, with rainfall throughout year. Temperature range generally between -6°C and 25°C. Coastal areas greatly influenced by sea. Winds cause day-to-day weather changes.

Deciduous trees lose their leaves in autumn when temperatures fall below 10°C, the minimum temperature needed for growing.

Deserts

Very low rainfall, less than 250mm a year. Daytime temperatures in hot deserts may exceed 38°C. Not all deserts are hot — some are cooler in winter, or even frozen (see polar climate, above). Living things have adapted to life with little water.

Tuareg herdsmen of the Sahara wear loose clothes to protect them from the Sun and sandstorms.

Tropical grasslands

Warm throughout year. Dry and wet seasons alternate, often with droughts during dry season. Temperatures between 21°C and 30°C. Scattered trees, with grasses over 1m high, which die in dry season.

Animals in the grasslands feed on trees as well as grasses.

Equatorial

Hot and wet all year round. High temperatures, never below 17°C. Climate provides ideal growing conditions for plants. Great variety of plant and animal species.

Cutting down and burning equatorial rain forests may be affecting world climates.

19

Rocks and minerals

The Earth's crust consists of layers of rock which have been formed over millions of years. The rocks on the surface are constantly shaped and worn away by water, ice and the wind, and by movements of the Earth's crust. There are three main types of rock, called igneous, sedimentary and metamorphic rock. Their formation and composition affect the relief, or landscape, of an area. They have an economic value as they contain fuels and precious minerals, and provide materials for building.

Minerals

All rocks are made of substances called minerals which vary in shape, size and colour. Most are made from a mixture of chemical elements, such as carbon, iron or silicon. Many rocks are made from several minerals, for example granite, which contains quartz, feldspar and mica.

Minerals may form regular, geometric shapes called crystals, for instance when molten rock solidifies or a liquid evaporates.

Diamonds are minerals of pure carbon, formed in an igneous rock called kimberlite in the upper mantle, under great heat and pressure.

Growing a crystal

Rocks are made up of many minerals and crystals of different shapes and colours. Below is an experiment with crystals which shows how they grow in size as liquid evaporates. Copper sulphate (from a chemist) is best to use.

Copper sulphate

Take care with copper sulphate, as it is mildly poisonous.

1. Pour 200ml of warm water into a jar. Add some copper sulphate and stir to dissolve it. Keep on adding until no more will dissolve (it sinks to the bottom).

Warm water

Jar

2. Pour the solution into a clean jar, leaving behind the undissolved crystals in a small amount of solution. Let this evaporate, then choose a large crystal and tie some thread around it.

Crystal

3. Tie the thread around a pencil. Place this across the top of the second jar so that the crystal is suspended in the solution.

Jar — Pencil
Thread — Copper sulphate solution

4. Leave in a warm place. Your crystal will grow as the solution evaporates.

Igneous rock

Igneous rock is formed when magma from the mantle rises, cools and solidifies. If it reaches the surface, the landform created, such as a volcano, is called an extrusive landform. If it cools inside the crust, the landform, such as a dyke or sill, is called an intrusive landform. In time, as the overlying rock is worn away, intrusive landforms may appear on the surface.

Igneous rock contains closely-packed crystals, formed as the magma cools. Large crystals are found in rocks such as granite, which forms when magma cools slowly below the surface. If it cools quickly, minute crystals are formed, making rock such as obsidian.

A tor is part of a batholith which has been exposed.

When a vast amount of magma rises and cools within the Earth's crust, it may form a massive intrusive landform called a batholith.

Batholiths, often made of granite, may be exposed after the Earth's surface has been eroded away.

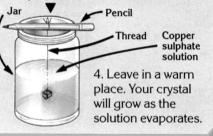

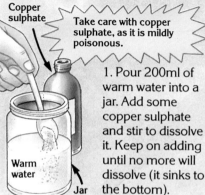

Batholiths may be hundreds of kilometres in area.

Sedimentary rock

Sediments are materials which have collected together as a result of natural processes. For example, when a rock is worn away by water, wind or ice, the particles may be carried away and deposited elsewhere, forming a sediment.

Sedimentary rock is formed from sediments. Layers of sediment gradually build up until the bottom layers are squeezed and cemented together, forming a layer of rock called a stratum. This process often continues, producing many layers of rock.

The weight of the top layers exerts pressure on the layers below.

Layers of sediment

The pressure squeezes the particles and they are cemented together, forming new rock.

Shells can be found in some limestone.

The type of rock formed depends on the nature of the sediment. Instead of eroded rock particles (which form rock such as sandstone), the sediment could be deposits left behind when water evaporated (which form rock salt). It could also be the remains of plants or animals (which form coal and limestone).

Metamorphic rock

Metamorphic rock is formed when igneous or sedimentary rock is altered by heat or pressure, or both. It can be formed in a small area, when magma comes into contact with other rocks, or on a large scale, such as during mountain building. Some examples are slate, formed from mud and a rock called shale, and marble, formed from limestone.

Extremely hot magma is forced into the surrounding rock (e.g. sedimentary rock).

The texture, colour and chemical composition of the minerals in the rock are altered by the heat.

Decreasing temperature

Unaltered rock

Slightly altered rock (metamorphic rock)

During the formation of mountains (see page 10), rocks are under great pressure.

The temperature of the rock may also rise due to the friction caused by movement.

Schist is a metamorphic rock formed during mountain building.

The pressure and temperature changes cause metamorphic rock to be formed over a vast area.

The composition of rocks

The arrangement and type of minerals found in different rocks give them certain qualities, which affect the way they are worn away.

Pervious rocks, such as limestone, for example, have cracks which let water through. Porous rocks, such as sandstone, have spaces between each tiny particle, and water passes through these. These are both types of permeable rock (see page 28). Impermeable rocks do not let water pass through easily.

In the Grand Canyon, in North America, layers of sedimentary rock, such as sandstone, have been revealed as the Earth's surface has been worn away.

The layers of rock have been shaped by the action of water.

The changing planet

When rock is exposed to the atmosphere, its surface is gradually broken down by various processes called weathering. There are two main types of weathering, called mechanical and chemical weathering, and most rocks are broken down by a combination of these processes. Rock material which has been weakened and broken off by weathering is called debris. It is carried away and broken down further by various forces. During this process, called erosion, the debris grinds against other rocks, breaking off more debris. Further erosion of debris may turn it into soil.

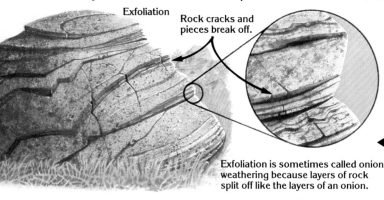

Exfoliation

Rock cracks and pieces break off.

Exfoliation is sometimes called onion weathering because layers of rock split off like the layers of an onion.

Mechanical weathering

In the day, the Sun heats rock surfaces and the minerals expand. At night, temperatures fall and the minerals contract. Most rocks contain several minerals, which expand and contract at different rates, making the surface crumble and break up. This is the main type of mechanical weathering.

◀ If rocks contain only one mineral, whole areas of the surface expand and contract together and eventually peel off. This is called exfoliation.

In cold areas, rocks which contain ▶ cracks, or fractures, may also be broken by a process known as freeze-thaw. If water enters the cracks and freezes, it expands as it turns to ice.

The ice exerts great pressure within the rock and forces the cracks apart. If the temperature rises, the ice melts, only to freeze again if it falls. In time, pieces of rock break off.

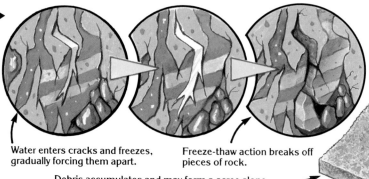

Water enters cracks and freezes, gradually forcing them apart.

Freeze-thaw action breaks off pieces of rock.

Scree slope

Debris accumulates and may form a scree slope. This may slide due to gravity.

The effect of freezing

By freezing some clay, you can demonstrate the effects of freeze-thaw action. You will need two lumps of moist clay (one to act as a comparison), some plastic food wrap and the use of a freezer. You can buy clay from a craft shop but try using some soil from your garden as it may contain clay.

What to do

1. Squeeze both lumps of clay to get rid of any air bubbles and make them compact.

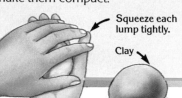

Squeeze each lump tightly.

Clay

2. Wrap the lumps individually in plastic food wrap. Place one lump of clay in the freezer and the other one on a window sill. Leave them there overnight.

Window sill

Freezer

Plastic food wrap

3. Take the clay out of the freezer and remove the plastic wrap. As the clay thaws, compare it with the lump from the window sill. The cracks in the thawed clay are due to freeze-thaw action.

Clay left on the window sill

Clay from the freezer

Chemical weathering

Chemical weathering occurs when minerals are eaten away by chemicals, such as those in rain. As it forms, rain absorbs gases from the air, making a weak acid which attacks the rock.

In rocks such as limestone, rainwater gets into cracks, making them bigger (see page 29).

Chemicals in rainwater attack and gradually eat away the rock.

Acid rain

Acid rain is caused by air pollution. The burning of fossil fuels such as coal and oil gives off gases containing sulphur and nitrogen. These react with water droplets in the air, making the rainwater more acidic.

Acid rain breaks down the waxy coating on plant leaves and also enters the plants through their roots.

Acid rain falls on the soil and enters rivers and lakes, killing wildlife.

Acid rain makes chemical weathering worse. In cities, it is causing serious damage to old buildings and statues.

Power stations release large amounts of gases into the atmosphere.

Clouds containing acid droplets may travel great distances.

Weathering by plants and animals

Plants and animals help to break down rocks by both mechanical and chemical weathering.

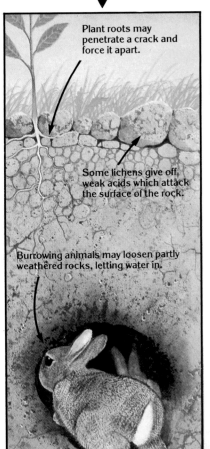

Plant roots may penetrate a crack and force it apart.

Some lichens give off weak acids which attack the surface of the rock.

Burrowing animals may loosen partly weathered rocks, letting water in.

Erosion

Erosion occurs after fragments of rock, or debris, have been produced by weathering. Agents of erosion, such as water, ice and the wind, pick up and carry away the debris. As it is carried, it is constantly grinding against other rocks, wearing away these rocks and being worn into finer particles itself. Finally, it is deposited in a new place.

Rivers
◄ Rivers carry a great deal of debris, which erodes the bed and the banks. When the river becomes too slow to carry the debris, it is deposited.

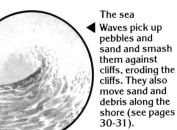

The sea
◄ Waves pick up pebbles and sand and smash them against cliffs, eroding the cliffs. They also move sand and debris along the shore (see pages 30-31).

Ice
In cold areas, ► debris is frozen into glaciers. As the ice moves downhill, the debris scrapes against rocks, eroding their surface (see pages 24-25).

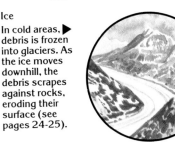

The wind
The wind picks ► up fine particles and blasts them against rocks, eroding the rocks. It has a particularly powerful effect in desert areas.

Speeding up erosion

Erosion has been accelerated by man's activities. For instance, soil erosion by wind and water is a problem in many areas.

Large areas of vegetation are cleared for farming or other reasons.

The roots of the plants no longer bind together the top layers of soil (see also page 37).

The wind blows away the topsoil, leaving barren areas called dust bowls.

Glaciation

During the last million years, the Earth's climate has changed several times. At certain times, it became much colder, resulting in ice ages. Areas of the surface were covered in ice, until temperatures rose again and most of the ice melted. The last main ice age was about 20,000 years ago, but some areas of the Earth's surface are still covered by thick, moving layers of ice, called glaciers.

Where glaciers are found

The largest glaciers are ice sheets, found in Greenland and Antarctica and in areas which have very cold winters and cool summers. Other glaciers, called valley glaciers, can be found in high mountain regions, such as the Alps and the Rockies, where there is snow all year.

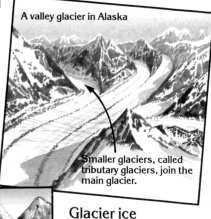
A valley glacier in Alaska

Smaller glaciers, called tributary glaciers, join the main glacier.

Glacier ice

Glaciers are formed when snow does not melt in the summer and builds up in hollows. The pressure of the layers of snow crushes the snow crystals and turns them into compacted ice particles, like snow which has been squeezed to make a snowball.

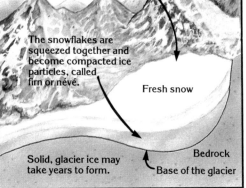

Snow builds up in a hollow.

The snowflakes are squeezed together and become compacted ice particles, called firn or névé.

Fresh snow

Solid, glacier ice may take years to form.

Bedrock
Base of the glacier

The moving glacier

Glaciers move because they are on sloping ground. The weight of the ice makes them move downhill, pressing on the rock beneath (bedrock). Their speed depends on the steepness of the slope, the amount of snow which falls and the thickness of the ice. Some valley glaciers flow as much 100m in a year, but in areas which are almost flat and have little snowfall, the glaciers (ice sheet glaciers) may only move a few millimetres.

In Greenland and Antarctica, ice sheets flow slowly down into the sea, where enormous blocks break off, forming icebergs.

Making a model glacier

As a glacier moves, friction is created as the debris grinds against the bedrock. This makes the ice move more slowly than it would do without debris. You can show this in a simple experiment, using two plastic containers (e.g. margarine tubs), some gravel or some rough stones, a piece of wood (approx. 45cm x 15cm), a cardboard box, a freezer and some water.

What to do

1. Half-fill your containers with cold water. Add gravel or small stones to one of them, so that the bottom is covered. Top up the other container so they are filled to the same level.

Containers

Gravel

Freezer

2. Place both containers in a freezer, making sure they are level. Leave them to freeze solid.

3. Remove the containers from the freezer and turn out your two glacier blocks. Before testing them, let them stand for ten minutes.

Glacier blocks

Ice

4. Lean the piece of wood against the box to act as your mountain slope and test both your glaciers to see which one moves more easily. You should find that your glacier with gravel moves more slowly because of friction.

Gravel

Glacier block

Cardboard box

Wood

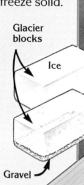

Erosion by glaciers

Glaciers erode and shape the rock they pass over. Valley glaciers, which move faster than ice sheets, have a greater effect. A glacier carries a great deal of rock debris, created in many ways.

For instance, freeze-thaw action (see page 22) occurs when snow melts and then re-freezes in cracks in the rock above the glacier. This creates debris which falls down and becomes frozen into the glacier. Pieces of rock are also plucked away from the bedrock by the moving glacier.

As a glacier moves, the debris grinds against the bedrock, wearing it away. This type of erosion is called abrasion. Spurs (see page 26) are also worn away, and the valley is straightened.

Erosion by a valley glacier

The ice erodes a steep-walled, saucer-shaped hollow, called a cirque, at the head of a glacier.

If two cirques erode close to each other, a sharp ridge, or arête, is formed.

Crevasses (deep cracks)

Debris is carried at the sides, in the middle and beneath the glacier.

Melting glaciers

The bottom layer of a glacier is nearly always melting. The water (meltwater) runs in channels beneath the glacier, depositing debris, called moraine. The front (snout) of a valley glacier is also constantly melting, due to higher temperatures at the bottom of the valley. Here, the meltwater forms streams which run out beyond the glacier. Normally, the snout still moves slowly forward, though, because the amount of melting ice is still less than the amount of new ice being formed at the glacier's starting point, or head.

In the warmer seasons, the ice may melt more quickly at the snout, and the glacier may retreat a short distance up the valley.

If this happens, the debris at the snout is deposited, forming a ridge called a terminal moraine. This marks the furthest point reached by the glacier.

Streams of meltwater

Snout

Evidence of past ice ages

At the end of the last ice age, the glaciers melted away, leaving large areas of the Earth's surface shaped by their erosive action.

Glaciated valleys are U-shaped, with steep sides and a flat floor.

Erratics are large boulders which were carried by the ice and deposited far from their original place.

Drumlins are low rounded hills. It is not clear how they were formed, but it is thought they may be the result of erosion and deposition.

Long winding ridges called eskers are formed from moraine. They were deposited by water flowing below the glacier.

Some scientists are concerned that if global warming (see page 15) occurs, the world's ice sheets and glaciers may melt. This would make the sea level rise and flood coastal areas, affecting millions of people who live near the sea.

A cirque may be filled by a small lake, or tarn.

Waterfalls cascade from hanging valleys, left high on the valley side after the ice has melted.

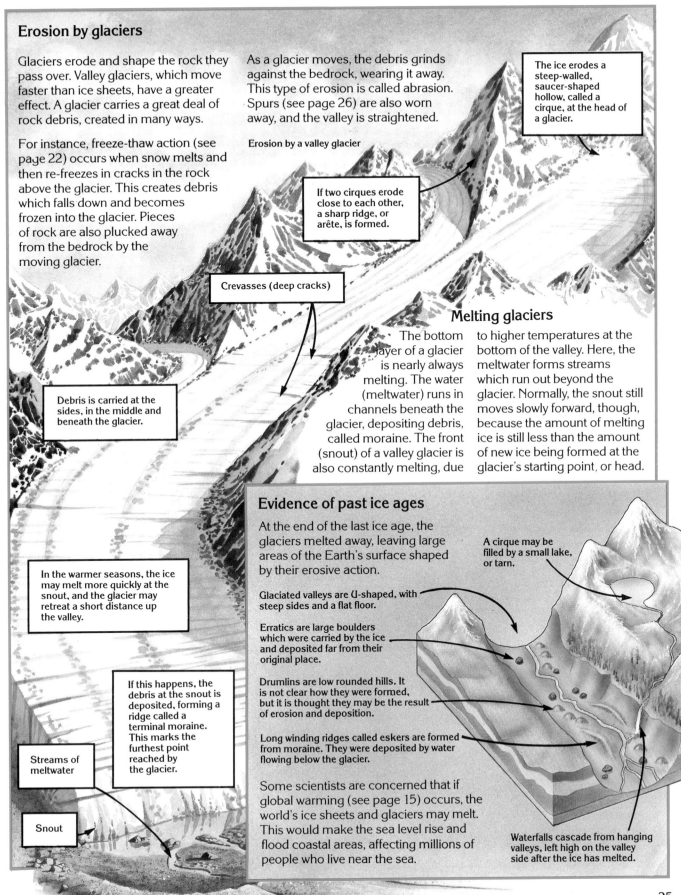

25

Rivers

Streams and rivers shape the Earth's surface by wearing away the rock they flow over and by depositing large amounts of material. The shape of a river valley changes along the upper, middle and lower stages of its course. Throughout the world, rivers are important for supplying water, transporting goods and producing energy.

Transportation and deposition

All the material (sediment) transported by a river is called its load. The heaviest rocks and pebbles are rolled and bounced along the river bed, becoming round and smooth due to contact with each other and the river bed. This process is called attrition. Finer particles of clay and silt are carried along above the heavier ones. They are suspended in the water. Some minerals travel in solution, that is, they are dissolved.

A river deposits its load as it slows down. The largest material is deposited first, followed by the smaller particles. The fine sediment may be carried as far as the river mouth.

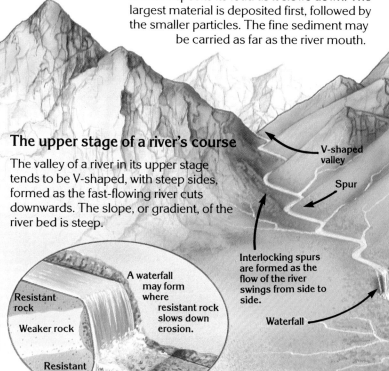

The source of a river

The beginning of a river is called its source. Many rivers have their source in mountain regions where water has run across the surface from various places and flowed into one channel. A river may also begin as a spring or flow from a glacier (see pages 24-25).

How springs are formed

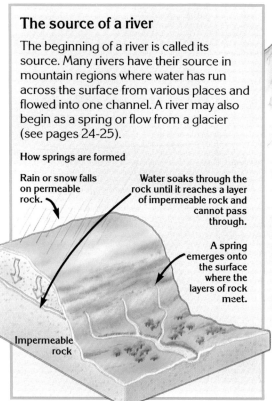

Rain or snow falls on permeable rock.

Water soaks through the rock until it reaches a layer of impermeable rock and cannot pass through.

A spring emerges onto the surface where the layers of rock meet.

Impermeable rock

The upper stage of a river's course

The valley of a river in its upper stage tends to be V-shaped, with steep sides, formed as the fast-flowing river cuts downwards. The slope, or gradient, of the river bed is steep.

V-shaped valley

Spur

Interlocking spurs are formed as the flow of the river swings from side to side.

Waterfall

A waterfall may form where resistant rock slows down erosion.

Resistant rock

Weaker rock

Resistant rock

Erosion by rivers

Running water erodes rock by the constant movement of the pebbles and particles of sand it carries. The amount of erosion depends on the volume and speed of the water, and the composition of the rock.

Most erosion happens early in a river's course, as the fast-flowing water carries large amounts of material. Some rock, such as sandstone, is eroded more quickly than resistant rock, such as granite.

River water loosens, lifts and carries away debris.

Rocks and pebbles roll and bounce along, wearing away and deepening the river bed.

Pebbles may be swirled around by the current, gradually forming a pothole.

Pieces of the river bed may be torn away if the force of the water is great enough. The water may also force air into cracks which weakens the rock. This is called hydraulic action (see also page 30).

River water contains chemicals from rocks and soil. It eats away the river bed and carries away the dissolved minerals.

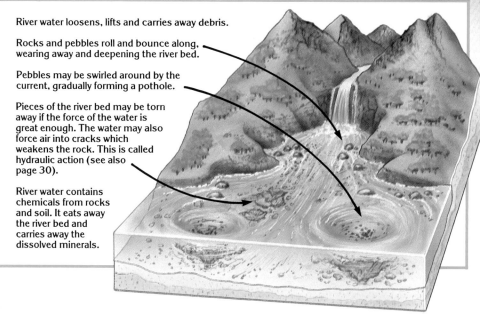

Pollution in rivers

Many rivers around the world suffer from pollution. In many areas, chemical waste from factories, and sometimes untreated sewage, is pumped into them. Rainwater falling on fields often becomes contaminated by chemicals such as pesticides. It drains into streams and rivers, killing animal and plant life.

Birds are poisoned when they eat contaminated fish or plants from a polluted river.

Looking at sediments

A river deposits sediment by weight – the heaviest first, followed by lighter and lighter material. You can show this, using a plastic bottle (1 litre size), about 60cm of plastic tubing, some soil, water, sticky tape and a plastic funnel (or one made from card).

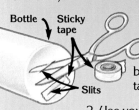

Bottle | Sticky tape

Slits

What to do

1. Cut two 2cm slits in the bottom of the bottle. Stick some sticky tape over each slit.

2. Use your funnel to half-fill the bottle with soil. Then almost fill the bottle with water. Screw on the lid, shake vigorously, and leave to stand for 24 hours.

Card funnel

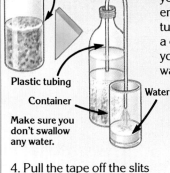

Soil

Plastic tubing

Container

Water

Make sure you don't swallow any water.

3. Unscrew the lid and place one end of the tubing into the water. Suck the water up, put your thumb over the end and bend the tube downwards, into a container. Remove your thumb and the water will drain out.

Bottle cut away

Layers of sediment

If the soil is very sandy, the sample will crumble. A clay soil will hold together well.

4. Pull the tape off the slits and leave for another 24 hours. This allows any remaining water to drain away. You should now see the layers of sediment. To look closely, carefully cut the bottle in half.

The middle stage

In the middle stage, the river's slope, or gradient, becomes more gentle and its speed begins to decrease. The valley becomes wider as the river erodes sideways.

The river begins to meander, or flow from side to side in long, looping bends.

The bends are also called meanders.

The lower stage

The volume of water increases in the river's lower stage, as other rivers, called tributaries, join it. It slows down, as the gradient is more gentle, and meanders across the valley floor, depositing sediments. Finally, it flows into the sea or a lake.

If the river floods, the water flows out sideways onto the plain and deposits its load, which is then called alluvium. The largest sediments are deposited first, forming banks or levees, which are seen when the water recedes.

The fine sediments are deposited over a larger area, leaving fertile soil after the water drains off.

Flat valley floor (flood plain)

Delta

Deltas

As a river flows into the sea, it slows down further, and any sediment it is still carrying is deposited. If the sediment is deposited faster than it is washed away by the currents and tide, it builds up an area of flat land at the mouth of the river, called a delta. The river splits up into narrower channels as it crosses the delta and finds its way

to the sea. This creates a number of islands of sediment in the delta. Many people live and farm on the fertile ▶ sediments which make up delta islands. In Bangladesh, millions of people live on islands formed in the delta of the River Ganges. They grow rice and keep cattle, despite a constant risk from flooding.

On several occasions, tropical cyclones in the Ganges delta have caused severe flooding, killing millions of people.

If global warming (see page 15) increases, the Ganges islands will also be under threat from rising sea levels.

Water under the ground

Rain falling on the Earth's surface may run into a river, evaporate back into the atmosphere, or soak into the soil. If the water soaks into the soil it may be absorbed into the layers of rock underneath, depending on their composition.

Water in rocks

Water travels slowly through porous rock which has tiny spaces between its grains, or through pervious rock which has joints or small cracks in it. Any rock which allows water to pass through it is said to be permeable. Water enters permeable rock and moves downwards due to gravity until it reaches a layer of impermeable rock (see page 21).

Porous rock, e.g. chalk

Tiny grains of rock

Water travels slowly through the spaces between the grains.

Pervious rock, e.g. limestone

Chunks of rock

Vertical crack (joint)

Horizontal crack (bedding plane)

Water travels along the cracks

Water storage underground

Water which seeps down through soil and enters rock is known as ground water. It stops when it reaches an impermeable layer, and the permeable rock becomes saturated (full of water). The highest level of the water in saturated rock is called the water table.

Any layer of permeable rock is called an aquifer. In some parts of the world, aquifers cover thousands of kilometres.

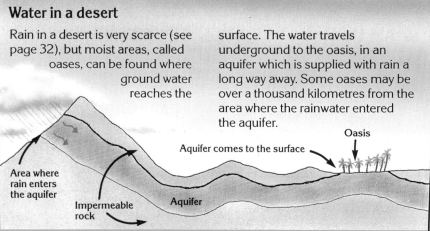

Aquifer

Saturated rock

Water seeps down

Water table

Impermeable rock

Rivers may be found where an aquifer is at the surface.

Bringing ground water to the surface

If a well is dug below the level of the water table, ground water soaks into it. If the level of the water table falls, the well dries up.

Normally, water has to be pulled or pumped up from a well, but if there is enough water pressure in the aquifer, water will be pushed out of the well. This kind of well is called an artesian well.

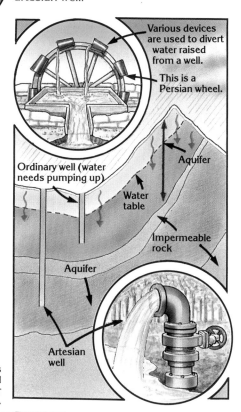

Various devices are used to divert water raised from a well.

This is a Persian wheel.

Ordinary well (water needs pumping up)

Aquifer

Water table

Aquifer

Impermeable rock

Artesian well

Water in a desert

Rain in a desert is very scarce (see page 32), but moist areas, called oases, can be found where ground water reaches the surface. The water travels underground to the oasis, in an aquifer which is supplied with rain a long way away. Some oases may be over a thousand kilometres from the area where the rainwater entered the aquifer.

Area where rain enters the aquifer

Impermeable rock

Aquifer

Aquifer comes to the surface

Oasis

Travellers in deserts often make long journeys to an oasis to collect food and water.

Limestone caves

Ground water, like surface water, can weather and erode rock. It is slightly acidic, having absorbed carbon dioxide both from the air and from the soil it has passed through. Limestone is particularly affected by ground water. As it passes along cracks and joints, the water dissolves the limestone, eating away at it and enlarging the cracks.

The cracks gradually widen, allowing water to flow as underground streams. The streams erode the limestone further by processes of river erosion (see pages 26-27).

The process causes areas of rock to collapse, leaving interconnected tunnels and caves within the limestone. Some water evaporates, leaving the minerals which were dissolved in it. These form features such as stalactites and stalagmites (see below).

Testing for carbonates

Any substance containing a carbonate (a chemical substance containing carbon and oxygen) will be dissolved by an acid. Limestone contains calcium carbonate, so it is eaten away by ground water.

To test for carbonates, you will need an old eyedrop dropper or an empty ball point pen tube (stick some tape over the tiny hole in the side), some vinegar (which contains acetic acid), a dish and some substances to test, such as rocks, chalk, sea shells or old snail shells.

Shell

Pen tube

Vinegar

Dish

What to do

1. Put a test ▶ sample in the dish. Dip the dropper or empty pen tube into the vinegar (put your thumb over the top end of the tube — this will hold the vinegar in).

◀ 2. Move the dropper or tube over your sample. If you are using a tube, lightly release your thumb, so the tube acts like a dropper. Let small drops of vinegar drip onto your sample.

Drop of vinegar

Be careful not to let too much vinegar drip out at once.

3. Watch your sample carefully. If it contains a carbonate, it will give off fizzy bubbles of carbon dioxide.

Carbon dioxide bubbles

Fizzing shows the presence of a carbonate.

Stalagmites and stalactites

Water is always dripping down from cracks in the roof of a cave or passage. It contains dissolved minerals, such as calcite. Each drop leaves a tiny ring of calcite on the rock as it falls. The ring grows as more drops fall, and becomes a hollow tube. If it gets blocked, water trickles down the outside of this tube and a stalactite gradually forms as it thickens.

The water which falls to the floor may evaporate, leaving a deposit of calcite which slowly grows up to form a stalagmite. Eventually a stalactite and stalagmite may meet, forming a pillar.

Chimney

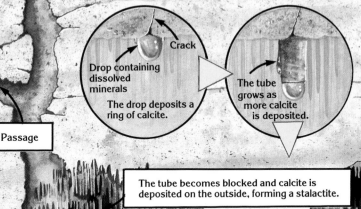

Formation of a stalactite

Crack

Drop containing dissolved minerals

The drop deposits a ring of calcite.

The tube grows as more calcite is deposited.

Passage

The tube becomes blocked and calcite is deposited on the outside, forming a stalactite.

If the tube does not become blocked, fine straw stalactites are formed.

Cave

Stalagmite

Pillar

Blocks of limestone where a roof has collapsed

Stalactite

Underground stream

The work of the sea

The waves of the sea have a powerful erosive effect on shores. Some shores are rocky, with high cliffs, others combine rocks with sand, shingle (small pebbles) or large pebbles. The breaking waves smash debris against the cliffs and also move sand and pebbles along the shore. The area between the high and low tide marks shows the greatest amount of damage.

Lines of waves usually approach a beach at an angle. This leads to a process called longshore drift. Sand and shingle are picked up, moved along the beach in a zigzag path and deposited elsewhere.

Lines of waves approach the shore.

Direction of the waves

Movement of the sand and shingle

The tides are caused by the pull of the Moon's force of gravity on the Earth.

There are two low tides every day.

High tides occur between low tides.

Waves

Most waves are caused by the wind, as it travels over the surface of the sea. The size of a wave depends on the speed of the wind, the time it has been blowing and the distance of open water it has blown across.

Crest

Near the shore, the sea becomes shallow and the waves slow down. Their shape changes to an ellipse.

Direction of movement

In the open sea, the water travels in a circular pattern, making waves.

Trough

The sea becomes too shallow for the wave to complete its full rotation and the top of the wave breaks.

As the wave slows down, it curves over and crashes onto the shore.

Erosion by waves

Waves are the main force of erosion on shores. As they approach a shore, they pick up debris from the sea floor and hurl it against the shore or cliff face. If the rock of a cliff face contains cracks, air is squeezed, or compressed, into them as the waves break. As the waves retreat, the pressure is released and the air pushes back out, shattering the rock. This is called hydraulic action. Debris is gradually broken down and rounded by the repeated action of the waves.

The continuous blasting action of the waves enlarges cracks and joints in a cliff face. eventually forming caves.

Headlands are formed by areas of resistant rock, which have been eroded more slowly than the surrounding, non-resistant rock.

Stack

An arch is formed as waves erode caves on both sides of a headland.

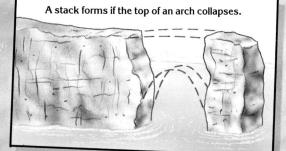

A stack forms if the top of an arch collapses.

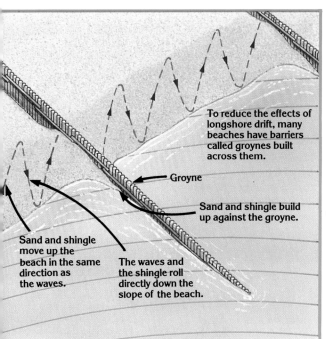

To reduce the effects of longshore drift, many beaches have barriers called groynes built across them.

Groyne

Sand and shingle build up against the groyne.

Sand and shingle move up the beach in the same direction as the waves.

The waves and the shingle roll directly down the slope of the beach.

Spits

Waves also help to build features along the shore. For instance, where the coast changes direction, or at a river mouth, longshore drift carries material straight on, off the edge of the beach. If the material is not carried away by strong currents, a ridge of sand and pebbles, called a spit, is gradually built up.

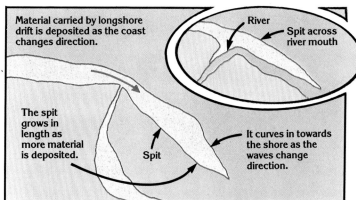

Material carried by longshore drift is deposited as the coast changes direction.

River

Spit across river mouth

The spit grows in length as more material is deposited.

Spit

It curves in towards the shore as the waves change direction.

Estuaries

An estuary is the tidal area where a river reaches the sea. Large areas of mud, deposited by the slow-moving river, are exposed at low tide, but covered at high tide. As the fresh water mixes with salty sea water, the salt makes clay particles in the sediment cling together. They become heavy and are deposited on the mud banks.

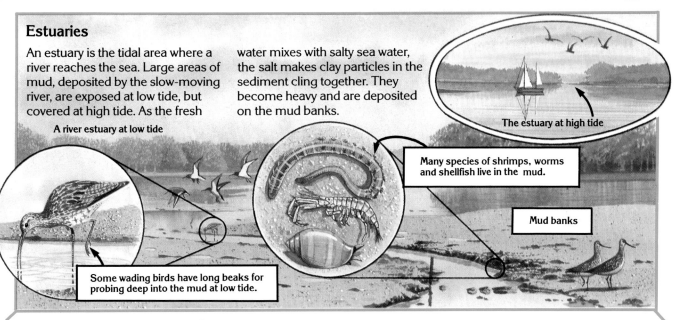

A river estuary at low tide

The estuary at high tide

Many species of shrimps, worms and shellfish live in the mud.

Mud banks

Some wading birds have long beaks for probing deep into the mud at low tide.

Fresh and salt water experiment

As a river reaches the sea, any remaining sediment is deposited due to it slowing down, but also because of the action of the salt in sea water (see above). This experiment shows how salty water speeds up deposition.

1. Put equal amounts of soil into the bottom of two glasses. Fill each glass with water.

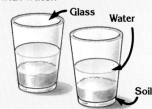

Glass

Water

Soil

2. Add two teaspoonfuls of salt to one of the glasses.

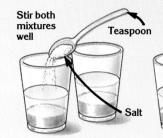

Stir both mixtures well

Teaspoon

Salt

3. Leave both glasses to stand. The salty water mixture will clear in a few minutes, leaving a layer of sediment on the bottom.

Salty water

Particles of soil remain suspended in the fresh water.

Sediment

Deserts

Deserts are dry, barren areas where less than 25cm of rain falls each year and the wind is the main factor in shaping the landscape. Not all deserts are hot – some of the world's coldest places are deserts. Desert plants and animals have special ways of coping with the conditions.

Where deserts are found

There are a number of reasons why some areas of the Earth's surface receive little or no rain.

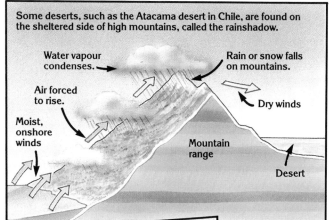

Some deserts, such as the Atacama desert in Chile, are found on the sheltered side of high mountains, called the rainshadow.

Water vapour condenses.

Rain or snow falls on mountains.

Air forced to rise.

Dry winds

Moist, onshore winds

Mountain range

Desert

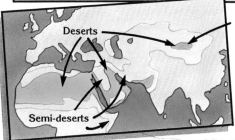

Deserts

Other deserts, such as the Gobi desert, are found in the interior of large continents.

Semi-deserts

Winds lose all their moisture as they travel over land.

Frozen deserts

Most of the snow in Antarctica and the Arctic falls at the coast, whereas areas of the interior receive very little, making them deserts. The snowfall is not very regular and most of the annual amount may fall during one blizzard. The snow has taken thousands of years to build up.

Most polar animals live near the sea, which is their food source.

Thick layers of fat or fur retain their body heat in the extreme cold.

Hot deserts

Hot deserts have a variety of different surfaces. Only some are covered in sand. Others have stones, gravel or bare rock, or a mixture.

Resistant rock

Layers of rock of different resistance

Direction of the prevailing wind

Wind action

There is little to protect a desert from the action of the wind. Strong winds pick up fine surface debris and blast it against exposed rock.

Most erosion takes place just above the surface, where the wind carries most debris.

Mushroom-shaped rock called a zeugen

In sandy deserts, the wind moves sand along the surface and builds ridges called dunes. The shape of a dune depends on the direction of the wind and the size of the sand grains.

The most common dunes are called barchans. They are crescent-shaped.

They are formed in deserts where the wind usually blows in the same direction.

Wind direction

They advance slowly as the sand moves up the gentle slope and is carried over the top of the dune.

They may be up to 30m high.

Seif dunes are long ridges of sand, formed when the wind blows from two directions.

They may be up to 100km long and 100m high.

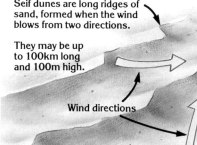

Wind directions

Temperatures

During the day, surface temperatures in hot deserts may reach 52°C, because there are no clouds to shield the surface from the Sun. It is much cooler underground, so many animals retreat into burrows during the day. At night, temperatures fall very fast, as there are no clouds to trap the heat and prevent it being radiated into space.

The fennec fox digs a burrow in the sand, where it remains during the day.

It hunts at dusk when it is cooler.

The fox's large ears have lots of blood vessels very near the surface. As blood flows through the ears, it loses heat, which is radiated into the surrounding air. This lowers the fox's body temperature.

Rain in deserts

Although hot deserts receive little rain, there may be occasional short periods of heavy rainfall. The water does not soak in straight away, but runs rapidly across the surface, sweeping up valley debris and carrying it along in channels called wadis.

Some desert plants produce seeds which stay buried for months or even years. After rain has fallen, they grow very quickly into plants. They flower and produce seeds, and then die off as conditions become too dry again.

When it rains, the desert is often scattered with bright flowers.

The seeds survived the dry conditions by lying dormant, or inactive, in the ground.

Many desert plants have a network of shallow roots which spread out over a wide area. The roots absorb any rain which soaks into the ground. The leaves are always very small, to minimise water evaporation from their surfaces.

Cactus leaves are sharp spines. Their size and shape minimises evaporation and their sharpness prevents them becoming food for desert animals.

When it does rain, cacti can store up the water in their fleshy tissues.

Cacti

Making a gerbilarium

Gerbils are desert animals which make popular pets. If you or a friend have gerbils, you could build a gerbilarium for them to live in.

Most pet gerbils come from the Mongolian desert, which is hot in summer and cold in winter.

Long legs allow them to cover large areas of land in search of food. They eat mainly seeds, stems and leaves.

Their long tail is used to give them balance when running and jumping.

In the desert, gerbils dig a complex system of burrows, to protect them from the very hot and cold temperatures and from predators.

Fur on the pads of their feet gives protection from the hot surface and also prevents them sinking into the sand.

Feed your gerbils on a diet of mixed seeds and occasionally fresh vegetables.

Keep your gerbils at room temperature, away from draughts and direct sunlight.

Do not disturb the gerbils in their nest.

Use a large aquarium with a tightly-fitting wire-mesh lid for good air circulation.

Put in dry peat moss, mixed with some straw, for the gerbils to burrow in.

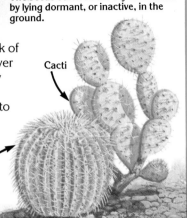

Fix a drinking bottle inside the glass and change the water daily.

Sucker

Small leafless branch for climbing and gnawing.

Minimum 20cm

For bedding, put in clean paper for your gerbils to shred.

The living world

The non-living environment (such things as the atmosphere, water, soil and rock), supports a wealth of living things. Different plants and animals, together with their environment, make up different ecosystems, such as deserts, temperate woodlands or tropical rain forests.

Everything in an ecosystem depends upon everything else for its survival, and each ecosystem depends on all the others. They combine to form the largest ecosystem, the Earth itself.

Food chains

All plants and animals need to break down food inside them, to give them energy for living and growing. Green plants take in the Sun's energy and use it to make their own food in a process called photosynthesis. Animals cannot do this, so instead they have to eat plants or other animals.

In any given ecosystem, the living things are linked by food chains. Plants are the first link in every chain. They are called producers, and are food for plant-eating animals (herbivores), which are called primary consumers.

An animal is called a secondary consumer if it eats herbivores and a tertiary consumer if it eats secondary consumers.

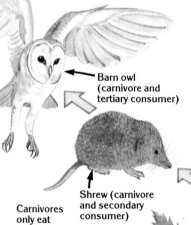

A food chain

Barn owl (carnivore and tertiary consumer)

Shrew (carnivore and secondary consumer)

Carnivores only eat meat (other animals)

Caterpillar (herbivore and primary consumer)

Green plants (producers)

Destroying ecosystems

When part of an ecosystem is changed or destroyed, other parts may be affected. If the primary consumer is lost from a food chain, for example, the secondary and tertiary consumers may die out due to lack of food, and the producer (plants) will spread rapidly.

All over the Earth, ecosystems are being destroyed, for example as land is cleared for farming or building. The destruction of ecosystems is causing world-wide concern.

For example, rain forests contain the largest number of insect and plant species in any ecosystem. They are being cut down at an alarming rate and many thousands of species are in danger of extinction.

Decomposers

In any food chain there are also decomposers, which feed on dead plant and animal matter. They cause it to break down, or decay (rot), producing various nutrients which enter the soil.

Bacteria, fungi and some insects are decomposers.

Studying decomposers at work

The main decomposers are bacteria and fungi. The air is full of bacteria, and the microscopic seed-like particles of fungi, called spores. You can try an experiment which shows that they are all around you, and in what conditions they will grow.

What to do

1. Put a slice of fresh bread on a table for a few minutes, to collect bacteria and spores. Cut it into four pieces.

2. Place one piece in each of three clear plastic bags (labelled B, C and D) and tightly seal the bags.

Plastic bags

Fresh bread exposed to the air.

3. Dry out the last piece in a hot, sunny place indoors. Place bag B in a warm room, C in a fridge and D in a freezer.

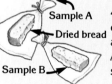

Sample A

Dried bread

Sample B

4. When the sample left out in the sun feels dry and hard, place it in bag A and place it beside sample B.

5. Observe your samples over a period of at least a week. You will find the spores grow best in moist, warm conditions.

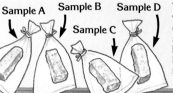

Sample A   Sample B   Sample D

Sample C

The very dry and very cold (freezer) bread should show the least growth of bacteria or fungal mould.

Food webs

There are many different food chains in every ecosystem. They interlink because each individual species usually eats more than one kind of food. The linking food chains form complex food webs.

A rain forest food web

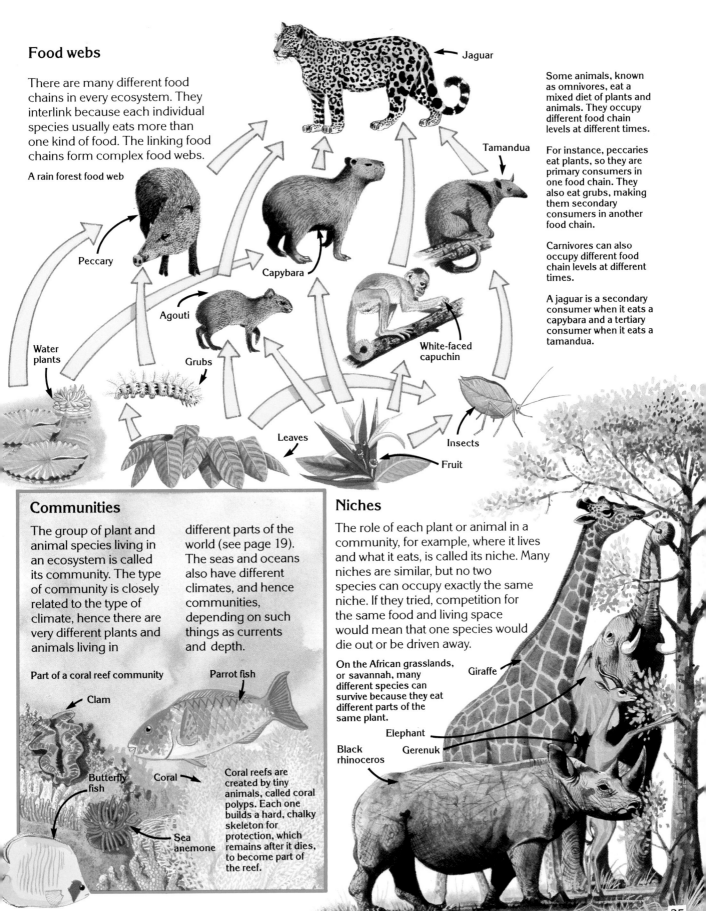

Jaguar

Tamandua

Peccary

Capybara

Agouti

White-faced capuchin

Water plants

Grubs

Leaves

Insects

Fruit

Some animals, known as omnivores, eat a mixed diet of plants and animals. They occupy different food chain levels at different times.

For instance, peccaries eat plants, so they are primary consumers in one food chain. They also eat grubs, making them secondary consumers in another food chain.

Carnivores can also occupy different food chain levels at different times.

A jaguar is a secondary consumer when it eats a capybara and a tertiary consumer when it eats a tamandua.

Communities

The group of plant and animal species living in an ecosystem is called its community. The type of community is closely related to the type of climate, hence there are very different plants and animals living in different parts of the world (see page 19). The seas and oceans also have different climates, and hence communities, depending on such things as currents and depth.

Part of a coral reef community

Clam

Parrot fish

Butterfly fish

Coral

Sea anemone

Coral reefs are created by tiny animals, called coral polyps. Each one builds a hard, chalky skeleton for protection, which remains after it dies, to become part of the reef.

Niches

The role of each plant or animal in a community, for example, where it lives and what it eats, is called its niche. Many niches are similar, but no two species can occupy exactly the same niche. If they tried, competition for the same food and living space would mean that one species would die out or be driven away.

On the African grasslands, or savannah, many different species can survive because they eat different parts of the same plant.

Giraffe

Elephant

Gerenuk

Black rhinoceros

35

The human population

Nowadays, there are more people living on the Earth than ever before. People create demands on the Earth and its resources, and have altered the natural environment to suit their needs.

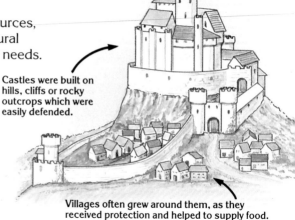

Castles were built on hills, cliffs or rocky outcrops which were easily defended.

The effect of the landscape

Since early times, people's lives have been influenced by the landforms and natural environment of an area. People settled in permanent communities in places where they could find water, food and a safe place to live. Many communities began near rivers, springs, wells or oases, or in areas which would not flood. Fertile soils and natural resources, such as coal, also encouraged people to settle.

Villages often grew around them, as they received protection and helped to supply food.

Population distribution

If all the Earth's surface was suitable to live on, there would be plenty of room for everyone. Large areas are unsuitable, however, so the world's population is unevenly distributed over the land of each continent. Few people live where the climate is too hot or too cold, the area is too mountainous or the soil is unsuitable for farming. Nowadays, most of the world's population lives in cities, towns or villages.

Houses in Indonesia are built on stilts to protect them from flooding during the rainy season.

Some people live in areas where they have had to adapt to unsuitable landscapes or climate.

Despite steep gradients, people in many countries have settled in mountain areas.

They cut terraces in the steep slopes to provide flat areas for planting crops.

A place to live

As the world's population grows, there is more demand for living space. It is estimated that the world's human population will grow to over 6 billion by the year 2000, compared to about 4 billion in 1980. In countries with large fast-growing populations, more people are being forced to live in overcrowded conditions or unsuitable places, such as on the islands in the Ganges delta (see page 27) or on boats in Hong Kong.

Hong Kong is so overcrowded that thousands of people live on boats in the harbour.

City problems

All over the world, people ► move from country areas into towns and cities looking for work. This is called urban migration. It causes many problems as the populations of the cities grow rapidly. There may not be enough homes, the streets become too crowded and pollution may increase. Squatter settlements, or shanty towns, may build up on the edges of the cities.

Changing the natural environment

Since early times, people have changed the environment for their own use, for example by clearing land for farming. When the world's population was low, this did not seriously alter ecosystems. But the demands of a growing population have caused great changes.

Natural landscapes and ecosystems have been destroyed to provide land for building cities and transport routes, and to grow more and more crops for food. Huge areas of forest have been destroyed, natural wetlands drained and dry areas watered artificially (irrigated).

Desert area

Irrigation channels

Crops such as dates and figs can be grown in desert areas with the aid of irrigation.

These, and many other actions, have caused great problems. For instance, in many places, cleared land has lost its fertile topsoil through wind or water erosion. This is called soil erosion (see page 23). It leaves unfertile soil, on which less food can be grown. In some areas, soil erosion, combined with drought, has led to famines.

In 1985, 30 million people in Africa were threatened with starvation which was the result of a series of droughts and soil erosion.

A great deal of their land has been left infertile by over-working and soil erosion.

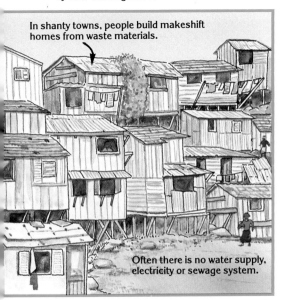

In shanty towns, people build makeshift homes from waste materials.

Often there is no water supply, electricity or sewage system.

How plants prevent soil erosion

Heavy rain washes away soil if land is cleared of its natural vegetation. For an experiment which shows this, you will need two identical plastic trays, a watering can with a fine spray, some plastic food wrap, soil and turf.*

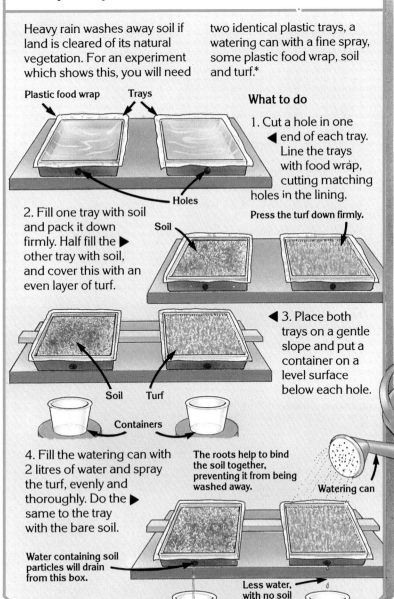

Plastic food wrap   Trays

Holes

What to do

1. Cut a hole in one end of each tray. Line the trays with food wrap, cutting matching holes in the lining.

2. Fill one tray with soil and pack it down firmly. Half fill the other tray with soil, and cover this with an even layer of turf.

Soil

Press the turf down firmly.

3. Place both trays on a gentle slope and put a container on a level surface below each hole.

Soil   Turf

Containers

4. Fill the watering can with 2 litres of water and spray the turf, evenly and thoroughly. Do the same to the tray with the bare soil.

The roots help to bind the soil together, preventing it from being washed away.

Watering can

Water containing soil particles will drain from this box.

Less water, with no soil

*If you are unable to find some turf, you could grow a tray of cress, but leave it for 12 to 14 days, to allow the roots to bind the soil together.

The Earth's energy resources

Most of the energy we use, for example in homes and industry, is taken from the Earth. For instance, wood is burnt to provide heat and light in many less-developed countries, and fossil fuels, such as coal, oil and gas, are burnt to produce electricity for use in the developed world.

When fossil fuels are used up, they cannot be renewed, or made again, in our lifetime. People are now beginning to investigate energy sources which will not run out.

Fossil fuels

Coal, oil and natural gas are non-renewable energy resources. They were formed from the remains of plants and animals that died millions of years ago. They are taken from the Earth and used in power stations to generate electricity.

The use of fossil fuels as a major source of energy has problems. At the present rate of consumption, known oil and gas reserves could run out within the next fifty years, with coal reserves lasting for about 250 years. Also, burning fossil fuels releases gases which contribute to acid rain and the greenhouse effect.

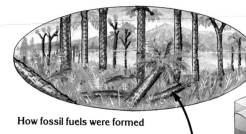

How fossil fuels were formed

Oil and gas were formed from the remains of microscopic marine plants and animals.

Coal comes from the remains of plants which lived in swamps.

Renewable sources

As the world's population grows and more energy is needed, many countries are developing the use of renewable energy sources – sources which will not run out, such as the Sun, wind and water. The idea is particularly popular because these are "clean" sources, and their use would not damage the environment.

Water power

The force of moving water has been used for centuries to turn water wheels to provide power for various tasks. Nowadays, huge dams and reservoirs are built so that it can be used to generate electricity, called hydro-electricity.

Solar power

The amount of energy which the Earth receives from the Sun is enormous. Modern technology has enabled scientists to develop ways of using this energy to produce solar power.

The world's largest solar power plant is in the Mojave desert in California.

It provides about 2,000 homes with all their energy needs.

The mirrors reflect the Sun's heat to a central boiler, containing water.

The water boils and gives off steam. This drives a turbine, linked to an electricity generator.

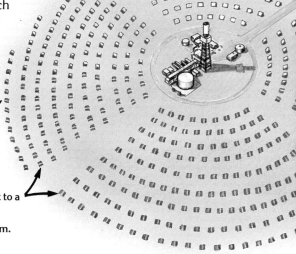

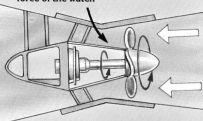

River water is diverted through a device called a turbine which is turned by the force of the water.

The turbine is linked to a generator, which produces electricity when the turbine turns.

A modern wind turbine

The wind turns the blades. These turn the shaft of the turbine, which is attached to an electricity generator.

Wind energy

The wind has been used as a source of energy for many centuries to power sailing ships and drive machinery. Many different devices have been developed to produce electricity from the wind, or to use the wind's energy in other ways.

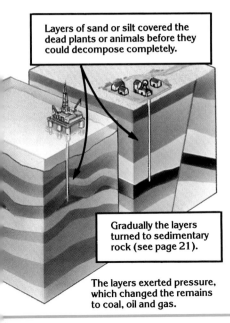

Layers of sand or silt covered the dead plants or animals before they could decompose completely.

Gradually the layers turned to sedimentary rock (see page 21).

The layers exerted pressure, which changed the remains to coal, oil and gas.

Nuclear energy

Nuclear energy is the heat energy released when tiny particles, or atoms, are broken apart. It is used to produce electricity. Uranium, a mineral found in the Earth's crust, is the main fuel used to produce nuclear energy. Many people think nuclear energy could be the main source of power in the future, but there are many problems attached to its use.

Nuclear power stations do not produce polluting gases. But nuclear power can cause several other major environmental problems, as nuclear fuels are radioactive. This means that they give off radiation which kills living things if they are exposed to it. Its effects may be disastrous if it is released into the atmosphere or into the ground.

There is great concern about nuclear accidents and the disposal of radioactive waste from nuclear power plants.

The nuclear accident in 1986 at Chernobyl, in the USSR, exposed many people and thousands of kilometres of land to harmful radiation.

Radioactive waste may remain dangerous for thousands of years.

It used to be dumped at sea, but most is now buried underground.

Strong underground vaults

Making a Savonius rotor

The Savonius rotor is a wind machine which is used by farmers in Africa and Asia to pump water for irrigation. To make your own rotor, you will need some drawing pins, a large plastic bottle, a plastic jar lid, two cotton reels, 1m length of 5mm dowel and two eyehooks.

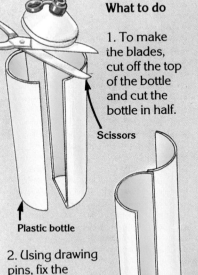

What to do

1. To make the blades, cut off the top of the bottle and cut the bottle in half.

Scissors

Plastic bottle

2. Using drawing pins, fix the halves across the centre of the lid as shown.

Drawing pin

Bottle

Lid

Take care when pushing the drawing pins into the lid.

3. Stick the cotton reels to the base of the lid and push the dowel into them.

Lid   Dowel

Cotton reels

4. Screw the eyehooks into a wooden support post where your rotor will catch the wind. Put the dowel through the hooks and test your rotor. Move the position of the bottle halves if necessary.

Once you have found the best position for the bottle halves, stick them to the lid using strong, waterproof glue.

Support post

Other renewable energy sources

In the future, many different natural sources of energy may be used to generate power. For instance, technology to make use of geothermal energy (heat energy from rocks within the Earth) is being developed in volcanic areas. Another source is biogas, a gas formed by rotting waste. It can be burnt to heat buildings and water.

Tidal power is already being developed.

Barrages are built across estuaries.

Reversible turbines generate electricity as the tide rises and falls.

Antarctica

Antarctica is a huge, cold continent, almost twice the size of Australia. It is the only place on Earth which remains relatively unspoilt by humans.

Most of the land is covered by thick ice, though coastal areas are exposed in summer and, further inland, a number of high mountain peaks are permanently ice-free. A variety of wildlife has adapted to living in the freezing conditions.

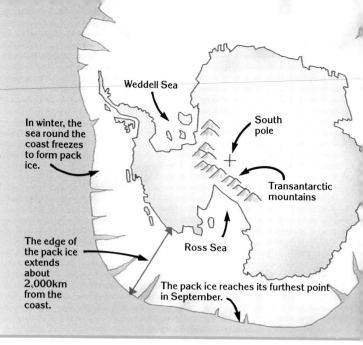

Weddell Sea

In winter, the sea round the coast freezes to form pack ice.

South pole

Transantarctic mountains

Ross Sea

The edge of the pack ice extends about 2,000km from the coast.

The pack ice reaches its furthest point in September.

The frozen continent

Antarctica is the coldest and driest continent on Earth. Over 99% of it is covered by thick ice, up to five kilometres deep. The centre of the continent is a frozen desert (see page 32), where the annual snowfall averages between 3cm and 7cm and temperatures range from −50°C to −60°C. Areas near the coast are warmer, with more snow, strong winds and temperatures between −10°C and −20°C. In summer, the ice around the coast melts, revealing narrow strips of rocky shoreline, as well as the islands around the coast.

Research in Antarctica

Scientists from many countries work in research stations in Antarctica, and on the islands around its coast. They study many different aspects of the continent, such as its weather, ecosystems, geography and geology.

They also monitor changes in the world's climates, levels of air pollution and the hole in the ozone layer above Antarctica.

Records of weather conditions are made daily by instruments attached to a hydrogen-filled balloon.

They measure temperature, air pressure and humidity over 20km above Antarctica.

Wildlife

The various birds and other animals which live in Antarctica need to be able to survive the freezing conditions on both the land, where they live and breed, and in the sea, which they depend upon to supply them with their food. They keep in their body heat with either a dense layer of fat, called blubber, found beneath their skin, or with very thick fur.

An Antarctic ocean food web

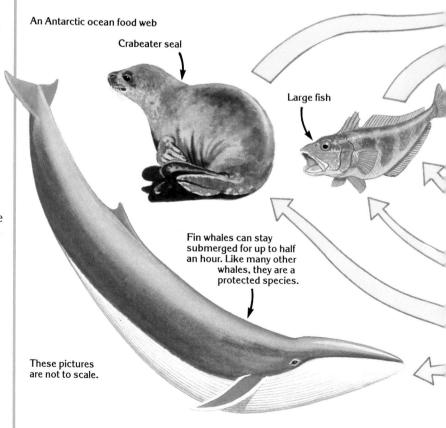

Crabeater seal

Large fish

Fin whales can stay submerged for up to half an hour. Like many other whales, they are a protected species.

These pictures are not to scale.

The Antarctic treaty

In the past, explorers landed in Antarctica and claimed parts of it for their own country. This led to disputes about which country owned which part. In 1959, a treaty was signed by twelve nations who had decided to work together to keep Antarctica free from exploitation. They have now been joined by many other countries.

Antarctica is the only part of the world ruled by an international agreement.

The treaty has helped to protect Antarctica's wildlife.

The scientists from one country must share their discoveries with all the other countries in the treaty.

The only military personnel allowed are those helping at scientific research stations.

Scientists use snow mobiles to travel across the ice.

Mineral exploitation

Geologists think there may be large reserves of minerals, such as coal, iron and copper, in and around Antarctica. Some countries wanted to be given permission to dig there for minerals, but the Antarctic treaty was reviewed in 1991, and any mineral exploration was prevented for fifty years.

Conservationists think that mining for minerals would endanger the animals and plants.

Airstrips and quays would be built in areas which are ice-free in summer.

These are the places where most seal, penguin and seabird colonies are found.

Greenpeace in Antarctica

Greenpeace, the environmental group, has its own research base in Antarctica. Along with many other groups, it is concerned about the future of the continent.

Greenpeace's aim is to make Antarctica a world park, with the plants and animals protected and human activities limited and controlled. They think scientific research should continue, but they are campaigning against mineral exploration and the use of Antarctica for military purposes.

Greenpeace workers in Antarctica are constantly fighting to protect its natural ecosystems.

For instance, they have protested against the construction of an airstrip and collected rubbish left lying around a research base, which they delivered to the base commander. They are also continuing their fight against whaling.

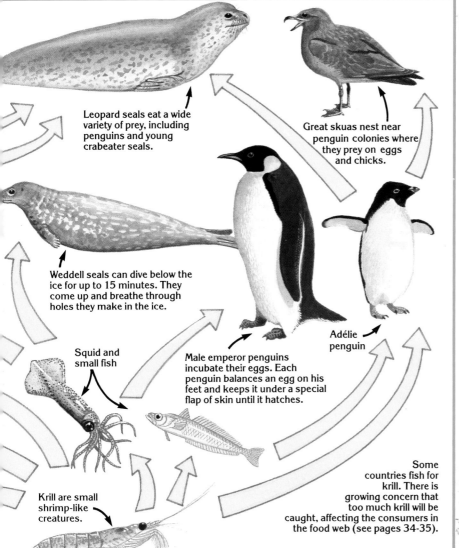

Leopard seals eat a wide variety of prey, including penguins and young crabeater seals.

Great skuas nest near penguin colonies where they prey on eggs and chicks.

Weddell seals can dive below the ice for up to 15 minutes. They come up and breathe through holes they make in the ice.

Squid and small fish

Male emperor penguins incubate their eggs. Each penguin balances an egg on his feet and keeps it under a special flap of skin until it hatches.

Adélie penguin

Krill are small shrimp-like creatures.

Some countries fish for krill. There is growing concern that too much krill will be caught, affecting the consumers in the food web (see pages 34-35).

Controlling the future

In some ways, it is difficult to tell what will happen to the Earth in the future. Natural events and disasters, such as earthquakes, floods and hurricanes are hard to predict accurately.

There are, however, many present-day environmental problems, such as global warming, which have been caused directly by man's activities. In these cases, we are able to predict the disastrous effects of allowing these to continue. We must act together to solve them if the planet is going to be a pleasant place in the future.

World problems

When the world's human population was much smaller, the Earth's natural resources could be exploited without affecting the environment. But now the population is growing so quickly that the demand for fuel, food and shelter is causing serious problems.

Acid rain, soil erosion, rain forest destruction and the threat of global warming are only a few of today's environmental problems. Much can be done to reduce or even solve them, but it will need the co-operation of people and governments around the world.

There are many ways in which action on a large-scale will help the environment.

For instance, if the destruction of rain forests, woodlands and marshes is stopped, many wildlife ecosystems will be preserved.

If there is a decrease in the number of motor vehicles on the roads, there will be less air pollution.

Car exhaust fumes contain many harmful gases, such as carbon monoxide and sulphur dioxide.

You can play your part in improving your environment. For instance, you could put your glass and paper waste into bottle and paper banks for recycling.

Recycling waste reduces the amount of resources taken from the Earth.

The oceans

In the future, the oceans are likely to become a major source of food and energy, so we need to preserve ocean ecosystems and halt the damage that is being done. At the moment, enormous amounts of household and industrial waste are being dumped directly into the water. Spillages from oil tankers are also adding to the pollution.

Cleaning up the pollution is vital if the fish and other sea creatures are to survive. Without them, there will be no food from the sea in the future.

At the same time, the quantities of fish which are caught will need to be carefully controlled to protect natural ecosystems.

Farming

As the world's population grows, so does the demand for food. Many international charities are helping to improve farming techniques in developing countries, which are often those with the fastest-growing populations. They have set up programmes to help farmers produce more food from the same area of land, to stop them destroying natural ecosystems.

Some new farmland has been created in desert border land. This land once had trees and shrubs, but turned into desert, a process called desertification, because of soil erosion (see page 37) due to overgrazing and the felling of trees, and unfavourable climate conditions, such as droughts and dry winds.

With the aid of irrigation, desert land can be reclaimed to grow crops.

The people grow crops, instead of relying on grazing animals for their food.

Irrigation in the desert has some problems. For instance, the water evaporates quickly in the heat, leaving salt deposits which make the soil too salty for some plants.

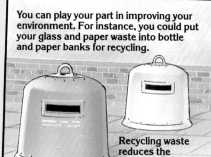

Making a model irrigation system

In many irrigation systems, devices called Persian wheels are used to divert water. For a model wheel, you need three plastic lids, 15 lolly sticks, a plastic egg box, strong waterproof glue, a cardboard tube from a paper towel roll, three pieces of wood (20cm x 5cm x 2.5cm, 20cm x 15cm x 1cm and 10cm x 4cm x 4cm), sticky putty, two pieces of 3mm wooden dowel (20cm and 23cm), four 5mm cable clips and some foil.

Ask an adult to help you make holes in the lids and hammer in the clips.

What to do

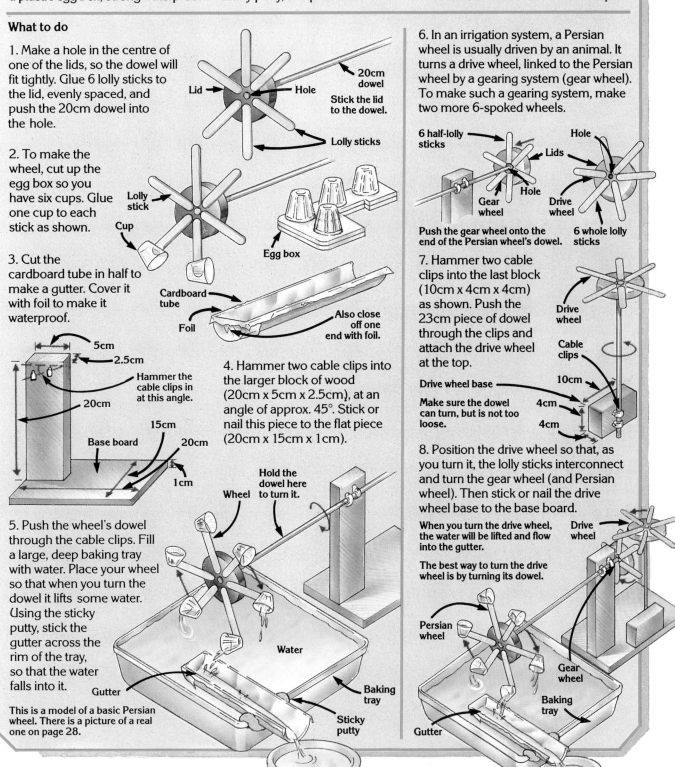

1. Make a hole in the centre of one of the lids, so the dowel will fit tightly. Glue 6 lolly sticks to the lid, evenly spaced, and push the 20cm dowel into the hole.

Lid — Hole — 20cm dowel — Stick the lid to the dowel. — Lolly sticks

2. To make the wheel, cut up the egg box so you have six cups. Glue one cup to each stick as shown.

Lolly stick — Cup — Egg box

3. Cut the cardboard tube in half to make a gutter. Cover it with foil to make it waterproof.

Cardboard tube — Foil — Also close off one end with foil.

5cm — 2.5cm — Hammer the cable clips in at this angle. — 20cm — 15cm — Base board — 20cm — 1cm

4. Hammer two cable clips into the larger block of wood (20cm x 5cm x 2.5cm), at an angle of approx. 45°. Stick or nail this piece to the flat piece (20cm x 15cm x 1cm).

5. Push the wheel's dowel through the cable clips. Fill a large, deep baking tray with water. Place your wheel so that when you turn the dowel it lifts some water. Using the sticky putty, stick the gutter across the rim of the tray, so that the water falls into it.

Hold the dowel here to turn it. — Wheel — Water — Gutter — Baking tray — Sticky putty

This is a model of a basic Persian wheel. There is a picture of a real one on page 28.

6. In an irrigation system, a Persian wheel is usually driven by an animal. It turns a drive wheel, linked to the Persian wheel by a gearing system (gear wheel). To make such a gearing system, make two more 6-spoked wheels.

6 half-lolly sticks — Lids — Hole — Hole — Gear wheel — Drive wheel — 6 whole lolly sticks

Push the gear wheel onto the end of the Persian wheel's dowel.

7. Hammer two cable clips into the last block (10cm x 4cm x 4cm) as shown. Push the 23cm piece of dowel through the clips and attach the drive wheel at the top.

Drive wheel — Cable clips — 10cm — 4cm — 4cm

Drive wheel base

Make sure the dowel can turn, but is not too loose.

8. Position the drive wheel so that, as you turn it, the lolly sticks interconnect and turn the gear wheel (and Persian wheel). Then stick or nail the drive wheel base to the base board.

When you turn the drive wheel, the water will be lifted and flow into the gutter.

The best way to turn the drive wheel is by turning its dowel.

Drive wheel — Persian wheel — Gear wheel — Baking tray — Gutter

Earth facts

The Earth is not a true sphere. It is slightly flattened at the poles. The distance around the Greenwich meridian (see below) is estimated to be 40,007km, whereas around the equator it is 40,075km.

The total area of the Earth's surface is estimated to be 510 million square kilometres. The area covered by water is approximately 361 million square kilometres.

Lines of longitude are imaginary lines which run through the north and south poles. They are used on maps and charts to measure distance in degrees east or west of the Greenwich meridian.

Lines of latitude are imaginary lines which run around the Earth, parallel to the equator. They are used on maps and charts to measure distance in degrees north or south of the equator.

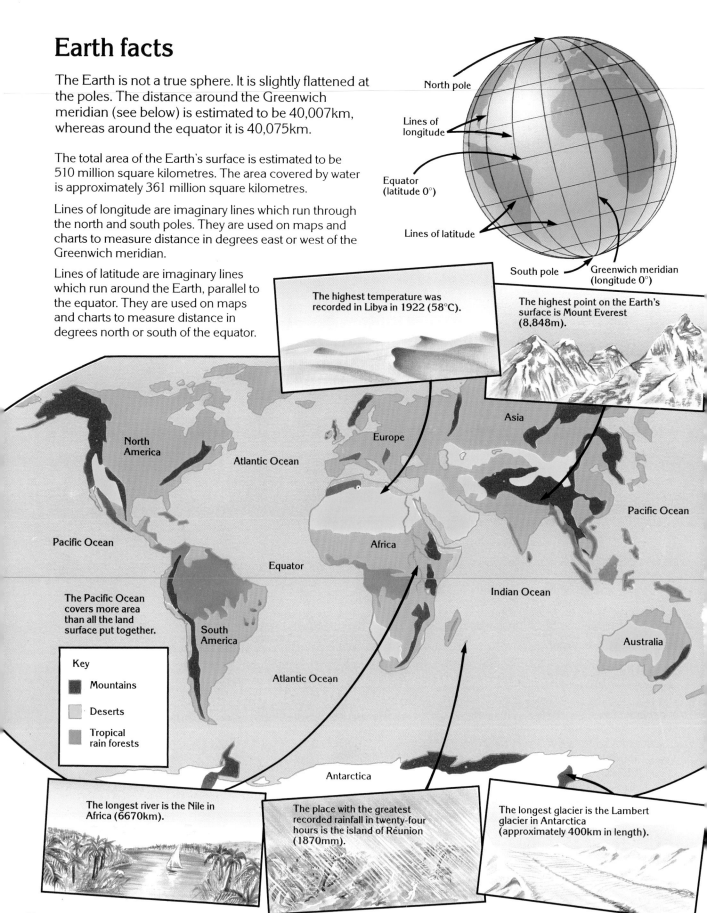

North pole

Lines of longitude

Equator (latitude 0°)

Lines of latitude

South pole

Greenwich meridian (longitude 0°)

The highest temperature was recorded in Libya in 1922 (58°C).

The highest point on the Earth's surface is Mount Everest (8,848m).

Asia

Europe

North America

Atlantic Ocean

Pacific Ocean

Pacific Ocean

Africa

Equator

Indian Ocean

The Pacific Ocean covers more area than all the land surface put together.

South America

Australia

Atlantic Ocean

Key

- ■ Mountains
- ▫ Deserts
- ▪ Tropical rain forests

Antarctica

The longest river is the Nile in Africa (6670km).

The place with the greatest recorded rainfall in twenty-four hours is the island of Réunion (1870mm).

The longest glacier is the Lambert glacier in Antarctica (approximately 400km in length).

Useful addresses

Below are some addresses of museums which have departments with permanent displays of rocks, fossils, wildlife etc. Your local library may be able to help you find addresses of smaller, local museums or suggest geological features in your area which you can visit. Also included are the main international addresses of some organizations concerned with the Earth and its natural environments. They may be able to provide you with further information.

International organizations

World-Wide Fund for Nature International,
Information Division,
Avenue Mont-Blanc,
CH-1196 Gland,
Switzerland

Friends of the Earth International,
26-28 Underwood Street,
London N1 7JQ

Greenpeace International,
Keizersgracht 176,
1016 DW Amsterdam,
The Netherlands

United Kingdom

The Natural History Museum,
(including The Geological Museum),
Cromwell Road,
London SW7 5BD

The Royal Scottish Museum,
Chambers Street,
Edinburgh EH1 1JF

National Museum of Wales,
Cathays Park,
Cardiff CF1 3NP

Leeds City Museum,
Municipal Buildings,
Leeds,
Yorks LS1 3AA

Manchester Museum,
The University,
Oxford Road,
Manchester MI3 9PL

City Museum and Art Gallery,
Department of Natural History,
Chamberlain Square,
Birmingham B3 3DH

United States of America

American Museum of Natural History,
Central Park West and 79th Street,
New York,
NY 10024

Denver Museum of Natural History,
City Park,
Denver,
Colorado 80205

National Museum of Natural History,
Wade Oval,
University Circle,
Cleveland,
Ohio 44106

California Academy of Sciences,
Golden Gate Park,
San Francisco,
CA 9418

Los Angeles Museum of Natural History,
900 Exposition Blvd.,
Exposition Park,
Los Angeles,
CA 90007

National Museum of Natural History,
10th Street and Constitution Ave. NW,
Washington DC 20560

Canada

National Museum of Natural Sciences,
Victoria Memorial Museum Building,
Metcalfe and Mcleod Streets,
Ottawa,
Ontario K1A 0M8

Saskatchewan Museum of Natural History,
Wascana Park,
College Street and Albert Street,
Regina,
Saskatchewan SP4 3V7

Australia and New Zealand

Australian Museum,
6-8 College Street,
Sydney,
New South Wales 2000

S. Australian Museum,
North Terrace,
Adelaide,
South Australia 5000

Queensland Museum,
Cultural Centre,
South Bank,
South Brisbane,
Queensland 4101

Museum of Victoria,
328 Swanston Street,
Melbourne,
Victoria 3000

The Western Australian Museum,
Francis Street,
Perth,
Western Australia 6000

National Museum,
Buckle Street,
Wellington,
New Zealand

Redpath Museum,
856 Sherbrooke Street West,
Montreal,
Quebec H3A 2K6

Royal Ontario Museum,
100 Queen's Park,
Toronto,
Ontario M5S 2C6

Provincial Museum of Alberta,
102nd Avenue,
Edmonton,
Alberta T5N 0M8

Glossary

Aquifer. An area of permeable rock which is capable of holding water and allows water to travel through it.

Astronomer. A scientist who studies the stars, planets and other bodies which make up the Universe.

Atmosphere. The mixture of gases which surrounds the Earth. It has a number of layers.

Backwash. The movement of a wave back down a beach after it has broken (see **Swash**).

Billion. One USA billion = one thousand million (1,000,000,000). This is the value used throughout this book. In some other countries, e.g. the UK, one billion = one million million (1,000,000,000,000).

Climate. The average weather conditions experienced in an area. Climates vary greatly around the world.

Continent. One of the large masses of land into which the Earth's surface is divided. The world's continents are Europe, Asia, Africa, North and South America, Australia and Antarctica.

Continental plates. The massive interlinking pieces which form the surface layer, or crust, of the Earth. They move around in relation to each other.

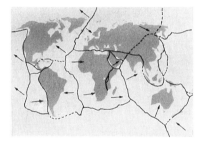

Debris. Fragments formed when weathering and erosion break down the surface of rocks.

Delta. A build-up of sand or silt, which splits up the mouth of a river into a number of channels.

Desert. Any area of the Earth's surface which receives less than 25cm of rain in a year.

Desertification. The process by which dry areas become deserts. It is a great problem at the edges of deserts where droughts have accelerated the process.

Drought. A long period of time with little or no rain.

Ecosystem. A self-contained system of living and non-living parts, consisting of plants, animals and the environment they live in.

Environment. Everything which surrounds a plant or animal, including the land, the atmosphere and other plants and animals.

Erosion. The wearing away and movement of material on the Earth's surface. The main agents of erosion are the wind, water and ice.

Faults. Cracks (**fractures**) which are lines of weakness in the Earth's crust and along which movement occurs.

Fetch. The stretch of open sea which any particular wind blows across.

Flood plain. A flat area which extends out on both sides of a river channel. It is formed from layers of sediment, deposited when the river overflows its banks.

Folds. Bends in rocks, caused by movements of the Earth's crust.

Food chain. A chain of living organisms which are linked together by their feeding relationships. Energy is passed on through each organism in the chain.

Fossil fuels. Fuels such as coal, oil and natural gas, which are the remains of living matter that died millions of years ago.

Glacier. A mass of moving ice which travels slowly due to the force of gravity.

Global warming. An overall increase in world temperatures, thought to be caused by pollution in the atmosphere effectively increasing the greenhouse effect.

Greenhouse effect. The warming effect caused by gases in the atmosphere trapping the Sun's heat.

Ground water. Water which has seeped into the soil and rock below the surface of the ground.

Humidity. The amount of water vapour in the atmosphere.

Hydro-electric power. Electricity generated by using the force of moving water. Hydro-electric power is one of the most widely used forms of renewable energy.

Ice sheet. A vast mass of ice and snow, sometimes called an ice-cap, which covers a massive area. Ice sheets are found in the Arctic and Antarctica.

Igneous rock. Rock which is formed when molten rock from beneath the Earth's crust cools and hardens.

Impermeable rock. Rock which does not allow water to pass through it easily.

Irrigation. The artificial watering of an area of land in order to create fertile land on which to grow crops.

Lava. Magma which has flowed out onto the Earth's surface.

Magma. Molten (liquid) rock found beneath the Earth's surface.

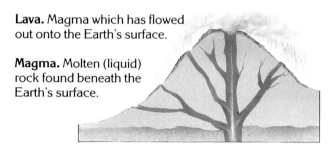

Metamorphic rock. Rock which has been changed from one type of rock into another by great heat or pressure.

Minerals. Naturally-made, non-living substances with a particular chemical make-up. Rocks are composed of one or more different minerals.

Ozone layer. A layer of ozone gas found in the Earth's atmosphere. It absorbs some of the Sun's harmful ultra-violet rays.

Permeable rock. Rock which allows water to pass through it easily. The water travels through spaces between individual rock particles or cracks in the rock.

Precipitation. Any moisture which reaches the Earth from the atmosphere, or forms on the Earth's surface. It includes rain, snow, sleet, hail, dew and frost.

Prey. An animal which is killed and eaten by another animal (the **predator**).

Renewable energy. Energy from sources which are constantly available in the natural world, such as wind, water or the Sun.

Sediment. Rock debris, such as sand, mud or gravel, deposited by the wind, water or ice.

Sedimentary rock. Rock formed from layers of sediment which were deposited and squeezed together.

Solar energy. The energy contained in the Sun's rays which can be converted into electricity using a solar, or photovoltaic, cell.

Swash. The movement of a wave as it breaks and advances up a beach (see **Backwash**).

Tornado. A twisting, funnel-shaped cloud, reaching down to the ground. Tornadoes create strong, spiralling winds which may cause severe damage, e.g. to buildings and trees.

Tropical cyclone. A violent tropical storm in which the winds circulate around a central point, or "eye". Tropical cyclones are also known as hurricanes, typhoons or, in Australia, willy-willies.

Tropical grasslands. Vast open areas of grass with a few scattered trees, found in tropical regions. Grasslands are given different names in different locations. For instance, they are called savannahs in East Africa and campos or llanos in South America.

Tsunami. A giant wave caused by an earthquake taking place beneath the ocean. It is sometimes misleadingly called a tidal wave.

Weathering. The disintegration of rocks by various processes due to exposure to the weather.

Index